AUNT JUICY'S
WAYWARD FAMILY

Shirley A. Franklin

"Aunt Juicy's Wayward Family"
ISBN # 978-1-7349886-6-6
Published by
Printed in United States of America. All rights reserved under International Copyright Law.

Cover Design: Hendro Wijaya

Acknowledgements

I want to first give thanks unto God and my Lord and Savior Jesus Christ for giving me an interest, gift, and opportunities to develop as an author/writer. I credit the Holy Spirit of God with giving me the inspiration to create writing projects like this one that were fun for me to do. I have created the character, Aunt Juicy, as a hybrid of a late great aunt of mine (Aunt Donnie), with touches of Tyler Perry's fictional character Madea and other aunts who I've observed over the years.

I thank my tribe, who helped me with the book in a variety of useful ways.

The information I found that helped me write about the real-life event, sometimes called The Jubilee, came from Wikipedia, Mobile Bay Jubilee at en.wikipedia.org and from YouTube URL https://youtu.be?NmeiUraECOc.

In writing about one of the special Bridge cousins, Benitta, who is an aficionado of high shine gowns similar to those worn in Ghana and by the 1960's singing sensations, Diana Ross and The Supremes. I grew up basking in this group's performances and admiring the way they dressed. I found source material about Diana Ross and The Supremes' dresses from https://www.motownmuseum.org/motown-sound/the-artists/supremes/.

Table of Contents

Acknowledgments 3

Character Profiles 7

Aunt Juicy's Wayward Family 9

We're Doing What For Summer Vacation? 15

Operation Be Good 17

Facing the Music at Aunt Juicy's 25

The Assignment 30

Laundry Wars 37

Aunt Juicy's Rant 43

Gardening Blues 54

You Get What You Get and Don't Throw A Fit 56

Hot Chip Madness 64

Private Meals and Secret Reveals 80

The Laziness Cure 87

Vacation Trip 92

The Jubilant Jubilee 104

Back Home 110

Epilogue: The Fate of the Bridge Family Characters 115

Character Profiles

Tania – 11 years old, petite and a bit scrawny, Tania is the main character in the story. She is tired of being accused of suffering from an eating disorder. She dreads a summer at Aunt Juicy's more than anyone else.

Aunt Juicy – Bossy and with razor sharp wit, Aunt Juicy loves her nieces and nephews, but considers them too spoiled and untrained. Her plan is to remedy this by having the whole slew of them at her house for the summer where she intends to "set them straight."

RayJay – Very independent, this 14-year-old cousin first gained Aunt Juicy's attention at the family reunion. It was because of his stand-out rebellion that she decided to have the Bridge cousins spend the summer with her in the first place. He finds out that Aunt Juicy is a force to be reckoned with. When there's trouble, RayJay is usually not very far away.

The Boston Beauties – Posh and sophisticated, the two sisters (April and Amy) have a very successful mother and enjoys the fruits of her efforts, although they don't spend much time with her. These spoiled girls add more flavor and mystique to the summer.

Terry – 12 years old, secretive, and mature, Terry isolates himself from most of his cousins, except Tania, during the summer at Aunt Juicy's. Like Tania, he comes away with some unexpected gains.

Baby Sweet – This 3-year-old little darling is always ready to give someone some sugar.

Benitta – 16 years old and foreign born, due to her mother of African descent (Ghananian). This cousin is a peacemaker. She learns a lot through the mistakes of other cousins. She also helps and nurtures the younger cousins. She has skills with a needle and thread, and with hair.

The Jazmines – All from Atlanta, Georgia—these three 13-year-old cousins are tightknit. They were all born to different parents of the Bridge clan, and all during the Spring (within 3 months of each other). One is a sweet, prayerful young lady, one is a huge nature-lover, and one is a bit obsessed with her telephone and other technology. They stick together and seem to have a silent signal system that no one else can crack. While they love their other cousins, they've had years to develop a true love bond with each other.

Brandy – With a head full of hair, Brandy did not come to understand how Aunt Juicy thinks and operates until after she arrives at her house. She is the first cousin to get a rude awakening at Aunt Juicy's house. An only child, the 11 year old learns about following directions through a very hard lesson on her first night there.

Elvin – 15 years old. He was jealous when his younger brother, Leonardo, came along. He doesn't want his pesky little brother following him, trying to be like him, or getting into his things. He always wants to show him that he is bigger and better at everything.

Leonardo – A smart 13-year-old, who encourages everyone around him, except his older brother, Elvin. He is always finding ways to irritate his big brother, and to prove to him that the bigger they are, the harder they fall, and he loves to make him eat crow for being so proud.

Aunt Juicy's Wayward Family

She was bossy, she was sassy, she was a champion investigator with razor-sharp insight, and she always had a jaw-dropping comeback. She could figure out what her nieces and nephews were up to before they could get very far in their many shenanigans, schemes, and mischievous plans. She was Aunt Juicy, and she didn't play. She had tons of wigs, hats, hair wraps, and various hairstyles and colors. This gave her different looks. However, her personality stayed the same. Her signature bossiness was a constant. She often said, "garblesnort," sucked her teeth or puckered her lips, as if she were sucking on lemons, when she was irritated or agitated. She cleared her throat when she was particularly annoyed.

Even though she had no children, she was quick to tell her siblings what they were doing wrong in raising theirs. Aunt Juicy was quick to criticize her siblings on their marriages too. She didn't try that nonsense with Ben, Tania's father and her own baby brother. Tania wondered why she and her cousins ended up with this aunt, out of all the possible aunts in the world. When this aunt told you to do something, she was surprised if you didn't immediately stand to your feet and get to it. This applied to adults as well as children. Tania had seen uncles, who didn't respond the same way with their own wives, jump up and run to do Aunt Juicy's bidding. These were most often her brothers-in-law, her sister's husbands and not even her brothers. Of course, she bossed her brothers around too. If she corrected you, she didn't apologize. She'd clear her throat and give you these looks that turned your veins to ice water, and then she'd say, "Hrmph," to express her dissatisfaction. When she gave you one of her unflinching stares, your decision to rebel or challenge her went right out the window. Tania wondered if Aunt Juicy ever told God what to do. Because she acted like she ruled the world.

She had been married for a long time, but her husband had drowned while swimming near the Gulf of Mexico. The story everyone was given was that he either hit a riptide or became too tired to swim back to shore. However, some whispered that he realized that he was going back to his bossy wife and decided not to return.

She never side-stepped the real, the truth. She didn't soft pedal when she had something to say.

Tania eyed Aunt Juicy as she perched on a hard, wooden stool that her aunt had brought to the family reunion. She had brought enough for all the nieces and nephews, which included Tania. She had explained, "Why these good, soft, cushioned chairs are for your parents. You know, the ones who go to work and provide for you, spoil you with video games, phones for ages 3 and up and other such foolishness? The ones who buy you things like Xboxes and iPads so that you can stick earphones in your ears and ignore them while you prance around all of creation with your fingers and thumbs constantly on some keypad or joystick as if they gave you life and sustain you daily. No! Ya'll can sit on these for the reunion. Now, don't let me see you sitting in an adult's seat. Starting with mine," she said as she slid her ample bottom into a plush recliner.

Her final words were confusing. "I love you so much that I could give you each 10 hugs and 10 kisses."

That's how the first full day of the Bridge's Family Reunion had begun. After an afternoon of watching her nieces and nephews try to order their parents around, ask for something 10 times after being told "no" once, harshly physically handle each other, fight over toys and gadgets, dodge any kind of work or effort asked of them, bump into people because their eyes were glued to their cellphones and didn't see what was going on around them, and whine about everything from the heat to the mosquitos to the television in their hotel rooms; she had called a meeting for every child 17 and younger. Not attending was not an option. She had made that clear after making an example of RayJay, who had bolted to his room like an ant escaping a boulder.

RayJay had a lot of experience with street kids in his Bedford-Stuy neighborhood. He was an urban child, a bit rough around the edges and used urban terms all the time. He was always calling things that impressed him, "Sweet." He didn't use such terms when he met his mother's bossy sister. She didn't seem like she was someone he wanted to be around, and she seemed to disdain anything but proper English.

In the meantime, Aunt Juicy had zeroed in on this nephew and then decided that RayJay would be her main project. She wanted him to learn some wisdom, and how to behave like a proper young man. So, she was not about to start the meeting without him.

Therefore, Aunt Juicy had showed up at room 517, put her finger over the viewfinder and pretended to be a food delivery service. She knew most of her family loved pizza, so RayJay had opened the door wide expecting a pepperoni with extra cheese. In she walked, and out he went a few minutes later, with her arm across his shoulder to steady him lest he try to go anywhere other than where she told him.

"No point in fighting me because I always win," she told him as they walked. "I'm the boss, Applesauce. No point in trying to pull the wool over my eyes either, because I have eyes everywhere. I have eyes in the back of my head, eyes on my shoulders, eyes on the back of my legs. So, even if I am walking away from you or have my back to you, I call still see you!"

In short order, every child under 17 was in the meeting room of the hotel, holding their breath as if they were about to plunge under water. It was at one of those worldwide hotel chains where the whole family was staying. The entire fifth floor was occupied by nobody but Bridge's. Even though Tania lived in Durham, North Carolina, where the family reunion was held that year, her parents had decided to join everyone else and spend the week at the hotel, rather than at home.

Aunt Juicy put her hands on her hips as she stood in the broad doorway and scanned the faces of her young nieces and nephews. "It's hard to believe that ya'll descended from slaves that worked 16-18 hour days in the hot, sweltering sun or brutal cold every day. They started at dark thirty, finished at dark thirty and got their fingers pricked and pierced and ripped by thorns - but they couldn't and didn't stop their backbreaking labor. You guys whine and bellyache over every inconvenience - if it's too hot or too cold, too windy. If an unpleasant smell breezes past you, or if someone says no to you or requests an ounce of effort from you; effort that will benefit you - you get all swole up with anger, offended for days and feel wronged to the nth degree."

Her eyes scanned the room, as she turned her head like it was on a swivel. She noticed Tania staring out the window, daydreaming. Tania had been struck with wanderlust again. Her impulse towards wandering was not quenched by the family reunion.

Aunt Juicy hitched up her flowered skirt with every kind of flowers in all the colors of the rainbow, squinched her almond brown eyes until they were like slits, spread her feet until each touched the side of the doorway and asked the collective brood, in her booming voice, "What's wrong with ya'll?"

Those 4 words were especially hurtful to Tania, because the saucy girls at school often started their teasing about her size with similar words. "What's wrong with you, Tania? Do you ever eat? Why are you so skinny? Are you trying to disappear?"

During the remaining days of the family reunion, Aunt Juicy had showed up like a party crasher, popped up like a bobble head, slid around corners like a shadow, stepped onto closing elevators and at different tables set up for the children on more than one occasion. She had corrected them when their parents failed to do so, and she had given them nicknames like egghead, apple head boy, peanut head boy, Mr. Slick, Hair Majesty, phone addict, Ms. Whiney, Sir Sleeps-a-lot, Never-Want-to-Grow-up Peter Pan and more.

We're Doing What For Summer Vacation?

When Tania heard the news that she and her cousins were being sent to Aunt Juicy's for the summer, she cried like she had been sentenced to life in prison without the possibility of parole. This news had come two days after the weeklong reunion had ended. Tania saw her parents' mouths moving to deliver this blow, and it felt like all the air had been sucked out of the room. It was like hearing that the family in New Orleans had been hit by a massive hurricane, or that a giant Sequoia had toppled over on her family's car while they were vacationing in California.

After she took a nap upon hearing the news and woke up to face the reality of her parents' decision, she called two of her cousins and then called her Aunt Juicy.

The cousins who she called were two and three years older than her. While she lived in Durham, North Carolina with both parents, they lived in Boston with their father. The cousins' parents had made an arrangement that enabled their mother to pursue a career in high end fashion. At the time, she was living in hostels and hotels in Paris, France and taking a college class in Textiles. She had sent her non-identical daughters, Amy and April, some purses that she'd made from canvas, nylon, silk and cotton. But that was 8 months ago, and they hadn't heard from her since.

"I don't like the way Aunt Juicy refers to mom and dad's arrangement as a "disastrous derangement." What does she really know about our family and our hearts for each other?" April was furious.

This got Tania stirred up. "I just hate the way she pronounces my name," Tania stated. She then removed her earbuds and put her phone on speaker mode. Every single time that these girls talked, Aunt Juicy showed up in the conversation.

9

It was hardly ever favorable conversation. The girls felt that she was too bossy and way too strict. "She's out of touch. She doesn't have children, and forgot what it is like to be one," Tania inserted. After bellyaching about the pending sentence to Aunt Juicy's house, they discussed some ways where they could convince their parents not to send them to hot Alabama for the summer.

They split the phone list in half, and Tania called half the cousins, while the Boston sisters called the other half. The Boston sisters lived in a neighborhood called Beacon Hill. "We're located on the Black Heritage Trail," they loved to boast.

Operation Be Good

As soon as the family finished any meal, Tania grabbed the dishes off the table and went to work washing them with ample suds up to her elbow. She also wiped down the countertop, stovetop and refrigerator door and handles; swept and mopped the floor and then cleaned the sink until it was a mirror.

On school nights, when her mother told her it was bedtime, Tania ran her bath water, brushed her teeth, finished her night routine in record timing and headed off to bed for the night. Her mom, or both parents peeked in the room to see if she were on her computer or phone, as was often the case. She was always lying in bed, still and quiet, with all lights out, and all electronic devices on the top of the dresser, which was across the room.

After two weeks of this, she noticed a sun shiny smile on her mom's face every morning when she walked down for breakfast. Her mother actually beamed at her, which she hadn't done in such a toothy way since Tania had read a Mother's Day poem that she wrote on Mother's Day. Tania had missed that glorious smile.

She reported to her cousins. "I think mom is starting to cave." The next day, when her dad brought in the mail, she had a letter from her Aunt Juicy. When she opened the pink and green envelope, her nose was hit with the aroma of roses. Several phone calls after she read the letter revealed that her other cousins had received the same letter. "It must have been one of those copy-and-paste jobs," her cousin Brandy had laughed.

Tania had not known what to do when she read the letter that she had not expected. She read it silently, and then out loud just to make sure she understood what her eyes were seeing.

Dear Tania,

I'm writing to you let you know my expectations and the best way for you to prepare for your summer visit from June 1 to August 17 (no exceptions except for academic or medical reasons like summer school or the flu).

1. Don't bring PlayStations or any of its games (and don't expect to use your phone to play games)

2. Bring plenty of good wholesome books to read

3. Plan on bringing pajamas with tops and bottoms, with no lace, thin material, tears or cutouts

4. Don't bring torn clothing, unless you plan to sew up all extra holes

5. Bring a suitable belt for pants

6. Sagging pants will not be allowed

7. Bring your Holy Bible

8. Bring your last report card

9. Bring raincoats and rain boots (no umbrellas)

10. Do not bring liquid body wash

11. Bring a cup or mug with your name on it

12. Disable all phone apps except Grammarly

13. Bring at least a 32-ounce bottle of sunscreen of at least SP30

14. Bring gardening gloves

15. Bring a straw hat

16. Bring stationery, postage stamps and envelopes

Please come expecting to get plenty of sunshine and exercise, and to do community service work. Come with an open, humble heart and mind.

By all means deary, come with love, cooperation and an obedient heart. MUAH!

With loving kindness,
Aunt Juicy

The cousins did a lot of three-way calls that night. They decided to step-up their be-good behavior, in hopes that they would get out of the summer sentence at Aunt Juicy's house. She felt that getting a letter that didn't have some X's and O's for kisses and hugs was a bad sign.

They text messaged each other with ideas that they thought of or that they tried. Almost daily, Tania got text messages from her cousins. They had content like, "I stayed after school and helped clean up after my class. My teacher said she'd give me extra credit." "I just helped my dad with the yard. He finished in half the time." "I got up early this morning and made breakfast for my family." "I babysat my little pesky brother for free."

Some of the best ones had messages like, "I gave my parents my phone this morning before school and asked them to keep it until this evening. They gladly took it. I told them I didn't want to be tempted to use it at school, which is against the rules. I've had problems in that area and my parents have paid $15 to the school a few times in order to get my phone back after it was taken up in class." Another cousin text messaged her about volunteering to take tutoring in Reading and Math twice a week so they could bring up their grades. RayJay messaged everyone that he was becoming a tutor for a special needs child with exceptionalities who lived in their neighborhood, and that he wasn't hanging with street kids as much. He reported that he was making his mother look good in their historic New York borough because she was proudly active on the social scene there.

"I made a mug with my name on it, and then I made one for Aunt Juicy with her name on it," another male cousin named Terry had written. Terry also let all of his cousins know that he had not gotten the same exact letter that everyone else had received.

Tania and the others could not get him to tell how his letter was worded differently.

"Based upon what you read to me from your letter, mine was definitely different," Terry commented. But that's all he'd say. Terry and his parents lived in New Orleans, having returned to rebuild their home after Hurricane Katrina. He carried a lot of personal pride as a Crescent City resident.

Tania was shoved and called a skinny anorexic girl twice in the last two weeks of school. She didn't respond. She just sighed and kept walking toward her locker. She knew she was not anorexic. She just didn't gain weight, despite eating plenty of delicious food.

She often ignored the girls who taunted her. Often, she escaped through daydreaming and wanderlust. Her parents, and friend Shelia often chided her for going off on bike rides and walks alone.

"It's not safe," her dad often lectured her. "These are different times. I don't want my daughter to fall into danger for wandering off to view the flowers at the Botanical Gardens, to ride the red Chance trolley, to treasure hunts to find 'caches' that are hidden around the city, to visit museums and go swimming – now I especially hate that one. You always swim with a buddy, that way they can get help if something goes wrong." Her father had put his palms on his forehead and asked, "What can I do to get you to stop this madness?"

She made up her mind to not get into trouble, yet she knew if the bullying behavior continued, she would need to report it to a teacher. She obediently promised to curb her tendency to wander off on her own.

If a teacher gave a good grade on an assignment, the cousins put it on their refrigerator while their mom and dad were within sight. Tania did it when her mom cooked. None of it worked. Well, none of it worked to get them out of a summer with their aunt. Tania did receive a manicure/pedicure for helping out in the kitchen without being asked, and for her good grades. She received a gift card to a jewelry and accessories shop and bought a few things while on a mall trip with her friend, Shelia. She even got a new dress. She didn't get out of the summer with her Aunt Juicy.

So, one Saturday morning, Tania found herself in the back seat of the family's SUV. Her dad drove expertly, following GPS directions, that got on Tania's nerves. They were headed from Durham, North Carolina to Fairhope, Alabama. She didn't sulk, but she didn't celebrate either. She put on her headphones and listened to some smooth grooves by John Legend. Her parents were driving straight through, and only stopping for food and restroom breaks. Tania napped a lot and played games on her phone before she was forced to delete them.

She went to sleep and awoke with a start. She smelled country fresh air, as they were driving down the driveway leading to Aunt Juicy's colonial style house. The driveway wound around the property in an S-shape. The property was full of old growth trees. Oak trees, sturdy and with wide trunks, dotted the property. Cypress trees formed a canopy to the right of the property. Just beyond it, if one walked far enough, was a spot of hidden wetland. When one came through the overlapping trees into a clearing to behold it, it was like a baby bird's first view from a cracked egg, gradual, marvelous, and assaulting to all the senses at once.

Flower beds, and creatively shaped landscaped bushes circled the perimeter of the property providing a barrier of varicolored wonder.

When they drew closer to the front door, a huge San Bernard approached the car. Tania knew that this would be her last-ditch attempt to avoid having to stay with her aunt. Her parents knew she was afraid of dogs. Tania deleted the game apps from her phone and tucked it into her backpack.

Aunt Juicy must have sensed their presence, because, without anyone calling to tell her they were there, or ring the doorbell, and without the lazy dog giving any notice; she threw open the door and headed toward the car with a 100 kilowatt smile.

"Radio," Aunt Juicy called to the big dog, who hung his head and walked away. "Get yourself to the barn, Radio," she ordered. Then she walked to the driver's side door and hugged her older brother. "Juicy," he said. He waited for her to move back and then got out of the car and stretched his long, lean body. "Come on, ya'll," he yelled to his wife and daughter. They exited the car, and then headed for the house. Tania was carrying her own luggage. That was new. Perhaps her dad had forgotten.

"Don't worry about Radio. He's spending the summer at a doggie den. They p ick h im u p t oday." A unt J uicy d irected t he c omment to Tania, who had just smashed a huge mosquito before it bit her arm.

Soon more low-flying insects made a beeline for her, as if sensing fresh blood and tender flesh. She swatted at them as soon as they landed, which actually stung as much as the insect bites. "Mom!" She yelled in a croaky voice.

"Oh, no, my allergies," Tania exclaimed. She hoped to get out of this trip. She dropped her luggage and grabbed a wad of tissue out of her purse. She blew her nose. Then she blew it again. She made a great ceremony of acting like the country air and foliage didn't agree with her. Surely her mother would insist on turning the SUV around and taking her back home, rather than let her suffer.

When she was 8, Tania had been afflicted wi th so me major allergies. She had been pricked in numerous spots on her young body, while her mother wrung her hands. After that doctor appointment of allergy testing, they had to avoid a lot of things. Plus, Tania had to take painful allergy shots and carry an Epi Pen. She was now 11, and no longer had allergies. She had been given a green light and clean bill of health two years prior, and again a month prior at the end of the school year. Still, she felt that her last-ditch effort was worth a try.

"Mom!" She yelled in a croaky voice. "Mom, help me." Her mother turned around and saw Tania in slight distress. Tania sighed and sniffed pitifully.

Her mother headed her way. Thinking t hat t he l uggage w as too much for her daughter, she took the handle of the abandoned luggage and headed into the house.

Tania unfolded her spindly arms, grabbed her backpack and then headed into the house. With every step she took, she wondered where had her mom's sympathy and white-knuckle concern for her health gone?

She noticed that the Cypress trees on the property let out such a strong, rich, piney aroma; as if the leaves had been pressed, cut, or crushed.

What had actually happened to them is that a super strong gust of wind had blown through about 10 minutes prior to their arrival and the trees had shook so much they sent a blast of earthy pine-like fragrance into the air.

When Tania walked down the sidewalk toward the house, she looked like a bride of an arranged marriage being forced down the aisle to marry a man she didn't want. Step by slow step she walked, hesitation and effort in every step.

As Tania ventured into the house, she gingerly touched tables, shelves and counters with different kinds of textured runners, cloths and colored mats with pots of Calla Lillys in the centers. She ran her fingers around the tops of the funnel style flowers. From the middle of each of these flowers arose a bright yellow cone with a definite likeness to a miniature corn cob with too much salt.

"Those are my Calla Lilliys. You like them?" Aunt Juicy had watched her niece moving her way slowly, captivated by the blooming flowers.

Facing the Music at Aunt Juicy's

Tania stepped further into the large, opulent house and her eyes took in all the beauty. There was a double spiral staircase and wraparound banister. The floor to the entryway, where she now stood, was made of tiles that shined and showed a polished reflection of anyone standing on them. There were hallways, and entryways and arched doorways, along with real crown molding and beautiful travertine flooring. Furnishings were high quality. Everything in the house was top shelf, modern, and neat as a pin.

"Shut the front door!" Tania spoke before she thought about what she was saying, and whose presence she was in.

Her aunt sucked in her breath. "The door, my dear, is already shut!"

Tania's mother spoke up and explained that her daughter had used an expression of excitement.

"Well, she should tame her tongue. I'm not used to these urban terms. I dare say, I don't want to become used to them," Aunt Juicy snorted.

On Tania's first night there, her aunt showed her the restroom assigned to her. It had a soaking tub and shower, a shelf full of colorful towels and plenty of toiletries and shower caps. It also had six shower caddies; one for each of the six girl cousins that would share that bathroom. Tania had a turquoise one. Her name was written on it in black Sharpie. After a dinner of an avocado and salmon laden salad and ice tea with a mint leaf atop, Tania took a nice soaking bath. She was ready to get out when she noticed that the huge fluffy bath towels were across the room. She called for her aunt. Sometimes back home, when she was in the same situation, she'd call her mother, who would gladly come hand her a towel from the bathroom pantry. Sometimes her mom would even help dry her back. Tania called and called for her aunt. She never answered and she never came. "I'll get it myself," Tania said out loud. She plopped one foot onto the floor, stepped out of the tub, and then stepped onto the carpeted mat to let her feet dry. Then she tiptoed across the room on the cold tiled floor and got her own towel.

Common sense and self-survival kicked in and she eyed the caddy her aunt had prepared for her. She realized that she should put everything she needed inside and then put it within reach for her showers and baths.

A cousin who arrived from Richmond, Virginia the next morning did something similar. In her haste, Brandy failed to put a shower cap on her head before she showered. When her ample natural hair got wet, she expected her aunt to take her to the beauty salon the next morning, like her mother would have done. Aunt Juicy saw things in a whole different way. "Baby, I provided you with a whole basket of pretty shower caps that I bought at the dollar store. It's no fault of mine that you didn't use what was provided for you." Brandy walked around with jacked up hair. She looked like she had stuck her fingers in a wall socket until Benitta, a cousin who also came from Richmond, arrived.

Benitta was the oldest girl cousin and could do any type of hair braid any time of day, anywhere. She regularly sported fishbraids, reverse or inverted braids, box braids, locs, cornrow braids, braided ponytails, Goddess braids, and something called Havana Twists. Her mother hailed from Ghana, West Africa and had taught her daughter braiding techniques from the time she was about 5. So Benitta, sporting a fishtail braid that trailed down her back like a kite string, had Brandy looking pretty as a picture with some cornrow braids within an hour.

Brandy never forgot her shower cap again, although Benitta referred to braids as protective styles that could handle water better than loose hair. Brandy even had Benitta show her a few tips for doing her own hair while it was braided, and for tying it up at night. "It's on your head, why shouldn't it be your responsibility?" That was Aunt Juicy's response when Brandy showed up for mandatory nighttime prayer with a pretty silk wrap over her head.

One of the Jazmines, used to having things like a grape popsicle and a cup of Mountain Dew for breakfast, had a hard time adjusting to Aunt Juicy's breakfast spread. They had oatmeal, mandarin oranges, and pineapple juice for breakfast on her first day there. This Jazmine didn't like the way the oatmeal looked and smelled, so she just sat and looked at the bowl as if it held the answers for all teenage problems and mysteries. She drank some water but wouldn't even lift her spoon. After everyone was finished with breakfast, she sat there looking at the bowl. Aunt Juicy required her nieces and nephews to eat what she put before them.

A chicken salad sandwich with a fruit salad and corn on the cob with lemonade was the lunch fare. Famished, Jazmine walked downstairs, expecting to eat some lunch. Aunt Juicy put the same bowl of oatmeal before her. She still couldn't eat it, so she just stared at the bowl. For dinner, Aunt Juicy prepared some grilled cheese sandwiches, sliced watermelon and a black bean salad with ginger ale. She wanted some of this dinner fare, especially the watermelon. When she received the same bowl of oatmeal for dinner, cranberries and cinnamon had been added. She lifted a spoonful to her nose and sniffed it. Her eyes lit up. Then she put the spoon to her mouth and tried it with the tip of her tongue. She loved it and ate the rest with gusto. She was still hungry enough to also eat half of the grilled cheese sandwich afterward. What she didn't know was that, after Aunt Juicy took the bowl of oatmeal out of the microwave this time, the other two Jazmines had doctored it up with the cinnamon and cranberries, mixed them so the flavors would bloom and then buried them just below the surface of the oatmeal.

Still, this experience was an eye-opener for the rest of the nieces and nephews. They knew that Aunt Juicy didn't play! She meant what she said and said what she meant.

Another Jazmine found out that, when they were given a schedule for trips ahead of time, they had to lay out their clothes and do all ironing the night before. They had to pass inspection, as if they were in the military.

Aunt Juicy told them this rule and posted it on the bathroom mirrors.

The Assignment

Aunt Juicy's Mary Poppins behavior showed up again when she gave the children an assignment that was to last for the rest of the summer. One of the Jazmine's showed up with wrinkled clothing, as she hadn't ironed her clothes the night before and a certain elf had removed all irons from the rooms. The embarrassed girl folded her arms across her chest to try to hide the wrinkles, but it only drew more attention to her disarray.

Throughout their experience with Aunt Juicy, they knew that she was going to give them an assignment to complete together because she had told them so during that first week. One Saturday morning in early summer, she gathered her nieces and nephews together in the den. "For these several weeks, we're going to go to a local nursing home and spend time with the elderly there. Then, we'll visit one of my elderly neighbor ladies and help her out around the house."

They already knew about the neighbor, Ms. Stout, as she was often in her yard or on her porch when they went by her house. As for a nursing home, they weren't aware of their aunt's soft heart toward this population. In short order, they were soon loaded into the SUV and pointed toward town. They arrived at Grey Manor and followed their aunt into the building. The walls were a nice shade of green. They were curious and cheerful by the time they got to the central area. A bevy of elderly men and women were inside. The seniors seemed to be expecting them. One older lady beckoned to Tania, and she looked at her aunt to see if she approved. She got a tiny nod and headed toward the crepe skinned woman with blue hair that matched her eyes. "Why you're such a pretty little thing," Tania was told. She chatted with the woman named Ms. Evelina. "Baby, I sure love the way you wear your hair," she told Tania. Tania told Ms. Evelina about a stylist named Beverly, and the older lady thought it was a super fine idea. "You're killing two birds with one stone. You're getting your hair done professionally, all while learning some things that you can do to your hair yourself," she said.

Aunt Juicy had the boys sit down the temperature-controlled cooler they'd brought into the building. They opened it up, and the juice, breakfast biscuits, sliced oranges, pineapples and kiwis were distributed to the elderly. While the grateful group enjoyed their food, the Bridge family sang songs of merriment to them. After a while, the elderly crew started making requests to hear specific songs. Some songs were sang by only Aunt Juicy, as the children, with the exception of the prayerful church-going Jazmine, didn't know many old standards. This left the nieces and nephews wondering if their mysterious aunt had ever been a professional singer. One old man with very hairy ears reached into his shirt pocket and brought out his harmonica and played an upbeat song to bridge the silence. Toward the end of the visit, the nieces and nephews were asked to give an impromptu summary of their favorite book. Tania got a kick out of this experience, as she had been reading a delightful book while at her aunt's house.

After leaving the nursing home, they visited Ms. Stout.

The scent of fish and seafood drifted on the breeze as they walked toward her house. The blends and layers of salt, sweat and sea filled the air, wafting on a current of fresh air. The aroma of piping hot fish and seafood filled the room when they walked into Ms. Stout's

house.

Right after the proper introductions, Ms. Stout brought out a hot apple pie and began cutting it and serving portions to the entire group. They chatted as they ate. She then showed them how to prepare and give speeches, by delivering one about the history of Fairhope, Alabama. "I don't have any chores for you today," she said. "But there will be some yard work for you boys and kitchen work for you girls next week," she cautioned.

"I have a weekly assignment for you," she announced with a twinkle in her eyes as she gave the details of the assignment. From that Saturday until the end of summer, she wanted them all to prepare and give a speech on a different topic, with props, every week. She gave them a handout on stationary paper. It gave some tips for preparing and making great speeches. It included using short, vivid words; using verbs that conveyed action; using rhetorical questions, using quotes, gauging your audience by mass reactions not the response of a small percentage; and more.

"Try to watch speech videos of Wayne Gretzsky, Governor Mario Como, Dr. Bryant Kirkland, and some of the flatbed truck speeches of Lyndon Baines Johnson." Ms. Stout had been a speech teacher for 35 years, and the necessity of the skill never left her thoughts. As she had already talked to Aunt Juicy about it, and secured her help, Aunt Juicy rose from her seat.

"I want to tell you guys about something that happens here in Mobile Bay called The Jubilee. Since Fairhope is on the bay, which is located in the Gulf of Mexico and on the Mobile-Tensaw Delta, sometimes salt water and fresh water mix in such a miraculous way that innumerable fish, shrimp, crab and other seafood flee to the shores and people catch them by the barrels, buckets, and washtubs full. There is more than enough for anyone who is already there or gets there quickly enough to get these natural freebies without effort. But you have to be quick, because the perfect conditions that create this ecological mystery often shifts, and the fish and seafood go back to deep waters and become elusive again." The children sat up, wide-eyed in wonder. Aunt Juicy described this ecological wonder so well, that some of them were picturing what this must look like. They were wondering if they would get to see this event, other than in their mind's eye.

Aunt Juicy told them the different nouns of assemblage, or collective nouns, used for the different sea life that washes ashore and almost begs to be caught during this early morning phenomenon. "You'll find shoals of catfish and flounder; beds of clams; arrays of eels; fevers of stingrays; troupes of blue crab and colonies of shrimp. I've seen their aerodynamic bodies thumping against each other and against the hard-packed mud on the shoreline as water splashed to the movement of their bodies created a symphony of sound in the southern sunshine. What happens after people have caught their bounty is that we have a great number of communal seafood feasts, broils or grills, fish fries, and clam bakes. Usually there's also many private crab bakes and feasts in people's homes."

Aunt Juicy told the children some of the circumstances that are perfect for this summertime blessing. Tania heard her say that the water near the shore becomes glasslike, and that the sky looks cloudy in a special way. She mentioned that the east wind will be blowing tenderly, and the tide would be ascending.

"About six days ago, we had a seafood dynamic, and Ms. Stout's man friend ran down when he heard the ship bell rang. The waters delivered a 15-mile-wide shoreline of easy to catch fish and seafood." The children were tiring of the scientific details, except one of them – RayJay, the Science fanatic.

But they became animated again, when Aunt Juicy went to the kitchen and brought out a round wooden tray laden with this fish, seafood with sides like zucchini slices, chunks of new potatoes, corn on the cob, and more. Along with that were long legs of blue crab, clams with the shells at half-mask, fat shrimp, slices of flounder and catfish. On the fringes there were halves of differently flavored corn on the cob, slices of lemon and shiny silver containers of melted butter.

"Line up and wash your hands," Ms. Stout told them as she pointed the way to the hot pink bathroom to the right of the dining room. The children bolted for the bathroom and queued up in a line to wash their hands with this rose scented liquid soap. Then they all headed to the long kitchen table where everything on the tray and more had been moved. When everyone was seated, Aunt Juicy said grace, and then had the children serve themselves as the tray with serving spoons, tongs and forks was passed around by Ms. Stout.

"Remember your manners," Aunt Juicy reminded them with a wink. Although she had taught them how to use silverware and even chopsticks; she hadn't yet taught them how to use seafood tools like the small double-pronged forks and picks to pry seafood out of their shells, and the seafood crackers that opens crab leg shells. She was proud of their strategies. They either watched her use the tools before trying, had another skilled cousin help them or sneaked their phones out and looked at video demonstrations with their cellphones hidden in their laps. Terry was an exception, as he was used to this kind of fare back home.

Later, as they filed out to Aunt Juicy's SUV, Ms. Stout handed each of the older ones a card with the requirements for their speech. It was like a criterion chart, or rubric.

At first RayJay was the only one who was passionate about the speech assignment. He taped the criterion chart on the wall and spent most of the following week preparing his speech and creating a prop that drove home his message. From his first speech to the last, he used a trademark beginning. "A lot of people know that Bedford-Stuy has a problem with..." He would name something like crime or such things. Then he would say, "But did you know that...", and he'd add some delicious additional information that balanced the negative with something positive and enlightening. This balance of weekly information informed the cousins that the late Congresswoman Shirley Chisholm and rapper Jay-Z were from there, that the Weeksville subsection of the neighborhood received recognition as one of the first free U.S. communities with freed African-Americans residents, that the borough was famous for its large outdoor murals called "Wallscapes," and that the life-robbing crack cocaine's heyday there ended, and that when he was U.S. senator, Robert F. Kennedy launched his "War on Poverty" program there.

During his speech on the first week, RayJay told them that famous movies by Spike Lee called, "Do the Right Thing," and "Crooklyn" were filmed in his hometown, as were some episodes of, "Everybody Hates Chris" co-created by Bed-Stuy raised comedian, Chris Rock.

Laundry Wars

Aunt Juicy still had these old-fashion ways of doing laundry. She had an arsenal of tools, including a bevy of cleaning solutions, stain removers, labeled spray bottles, wooden clothespins and a clothespin bag, laundry baskets that were color-coded, irons and ironing boards, and a variety of hangers to use according to her tradition.

On top of that, she separated whites, and used bleach for such clothing. She liked to add a little Pine Sol to some of her loads, but not all of them. She treated anything with stains with a special stain remover, and often put such clothes through two treatments before washing them. Bright colors, of which there were many, were washed in cold water with Oxyclean added on top of the regular special brand of liquid detergent for sensitive skin. Lighter colors were washed in small loads, and no explanation or exceptions were allowed. Anything red was washed alone when there was enough of them, but never ever after the whites. The delicate items were hand washed with powder detergent, and then hung on the line to dry. Anything run through the dryer was folded or hung on wooden or padded hangers as soon as the dryer stopped.

When the children acted like doing laundry was torture, Aunt Juicy put her hands on her hips and said, "Stop the whining. What's wrong with ya'll?" She did this a lot, because she was convinced that it was them and not her that had something out of whack.

"Don't be lazy," she often said.

The girls hated laundry day, which always started on Saturday mornings. The Boston sisters preferred preparing and giving speeches to doing laundry. They had decided on the first visit to Ms. Stout's house that they would talk about notable African Americans from Boston or who became notable in Boston, such as abolitionist and equal opportunity advocate Prince Hall, published poet Phillis Wheatley, speech icon and abolitionist Frederick Douglass, educator/

writer/activist/author and NAACP co-founder W.E.B. DuBois; who was the first African American to gain a PhD from prestigious Harvard University.

"First, we'll tell them about Beacon Hill and the Black Heritage Trail. Then we'll explain that in 1783 our state became the first to declare that it was illegal to have slaves," one of them said during one of their many brainstorms.

Still, they couldn't talk their way out of helping with laundry by saying they were working on their speeches.

Neither could Benitta, who had become a self-appointed guardian and hair stylist of the young playground set. She found out that most of the other cousins were taking the speech assignment seriously. She worked late in the night preparing organized folders of notes after she put the babies to bed. She put together a bulk of information about blacks during the Civil War era and about the former slave markets in Richmond, Virginia. She then pecked away softly on her laptop and took down notes about Jackson Ward, a type of Black America Wall Street and the statue honoring African-American tennis star Arthur Ashe. She found pictures and information about the city's American Civil War Museum at Historic Tredegar; about Richmond Community High School where schools were first desegregated in the city; and about the Richmond Slave Trail where slaves from Africa were unloaded from the ships, sold at auction and more.

Aunt Juicy had put her hands on her hips, let out an annoyed "Hrmph!" and then told them, "Children, why is everybody in here working on their speeches? You just have to manage your time and make some sacrifices so that you can get things done."

Many cousins complained to their parents later when they talked or sneakily did FaceTime.

"Mom, I was always able to sleep in on Saturdays. Can't you do something? You know how Auntie Bossy can be! If we try to sleep late, she won't let us, and she calls us lazy."

"Can I come home?" Another whiny cousin asked.

Others complained – "It's not fair!"

Still others cried, "This is supposed to be my summer vacation."

"We had to iron clothes that had no wrinkles. She has 3 irons and ironing boards in her hot laundry room," another complained.

Tania had it the worst. It seems that she was always doing something that caused her aunt to call her sneaky, lazy, whiny, immature, troubling, disturbed or a hot mess that needed to be put back in the oven until fully done. Aunt Juicy had actually told her that. More than once.

Tania's call was one of desperation. Two weeks after they all arrived in Fairhope, Alabama, Tania had spent $30 buying make-up when they went into the city. Aunt Juicy did a sneak attack on her soon after. She stood behind her, having sneaked up to her while she was admiring herself in the mirror. "Hey," she said in a loud voice. When Tania turned around, Aunt Juicy used the baby wipes and nice brown fluffy towel in her hands to wipe away all traces of makeup. Tania was mortified.

Later, when on the phone with her mom, Tania cried. "Mom, can I please come home?" She told about her aunt's warm, wet towel and baby wipe attack.

Three-year-old Baby Sweet, contented and clueless about the dissatisfaction brewing, walked around, visiting the different rooms and gave every sad cousin a kiss. Tania took her into her lap and gave her a hug.

Her mother never responded to her request to come home. She talked around it like a master dodger. "How's the weather?" she asked after one of Tania's long rants. "Sleeping in the country air does a soul good," she commented as Tania listed her aunt's many offenses. "Are you eating good?" she asked after her daughter shared how they were often sent out to the garden in the back yard to pull some cucumbers, onions, and tomatoes off of their stalks or roots which were still planted deep in the dirt.

"There's bugs, snails, and all types of creepy crawlers out there," she said. "Oh, and mom - we have to wear these big gloves, oversized shoes, sunscreen, and huge straw hats when we go out there. We had corn on the cob but had to go pick the corn off their stalks and shuck them. There's these fat silkworms on most of them. They're a fright!"

"I know Juicy has almost a million ways to make corn fresh from her garden. She makes creamed corn; she roasts them on the cob; she can make a salad with them; she microwaves them; she makes this Mexican corn-based dish called elotes by adding lime juice, hot sauce, mayonnaise, parmesan cheese and sour cream in corn. You haven't lived until you've had her corn."

Tania listened to her mother drone on and on and on like the Forrest Gump character as he'd listed all the ways you could cook or prepare shrimp.

After an hour, she hung up feeling a bit defeated. How much more would she have to take?

Aunt Juicy had a radar. Whenever the cousins had a Pow wow anywhere on the property, she would show up. Some of the cousins even began to accuse or suspect each other of snitching to Aunt Juicy and giving away their meeting times and places.

After this happened a few times, Tania noticed that one brainiac of a cousin would move off to some spot by himself and take out his phone and text like a speed demon, with his long piano-playing fingers flying across the buttons of his stupid flip phone. It was none other than Hurricane Katrina survivor as an infant, Terry.

Aunt Juicy's Rant

The cousins were sitting on the bleachers in the barn early one morning. Yes, she had bought some bleachers from a city school about 30 miles from her house when the school district purchased a new set of athletic equipment. Some of Tania's cousins had their pinched fingers on their noses to shut down the nasty smell. Baby Sweet was the only one who seemed not to notice.

"It's hot! How long do we have to sit here? Can we go back in the house?" One brave cousin asked this question.

Aunt Juicy responded, "You know you spoiled brats cry about everything. You can't stand when it's too cold. You make everyone's life a living nightmare if it's too hot. Nothing pleases you except being on your phones." Tania didn't think that was a fair assessment.

Tania looked up when she heard the din of complaints. As each had entered the barn, they had been required to surrender their phones at the door. They were on a table in buckets that had the phones nestled in plastic sandwich bags with their names on the front.

"Nice assembly," Tania said in her most sarcastic tone. She had turned around to vent to another cousin.

Then she watched as her athletic cousin, Terry, paced back and forth in the area across from the bleachers. When they had first entered the barn, he smarted off and was assigned to walk the entire length of the barn 12 times. Tania wondered, not for the first time, about the different content of Terry's letter.

The punishment or consequence had come about like this.

As the cadre of cousins filed into the barn, almost every single one complained about the smell.

"It stinks in here."

"This smells like do doo."

"OMG! This place smells like crap!"

"It stinks to high heaven."

They continued to whine and complain, bellyache and pretend to vomit or gag.

Aunt Juicy had watched and listened for about 5 minutes before raising the loud speaker to her mouth to talk, which Tania thought was ridiculous. Her aunt was a loud speaker. If you looked up the word in the dictionary, her picture would be next to it.

"I hear whining again, which you guys know I don't like. You're making a bunch of cry-baby comments about the stench. You're in a barn! What do you expect?" Just then, a cow started mooing. Everyone heard it and chuckled, creating a chorus of laughing, shrilly voices that echoed in the wide space. It dawned on Tania at that moment that they had hardly laughed that summer.

In spite of the cacaconophy of voices, although she stood across the room, Aunt Juicy heard Terry reply, "What we expect is for you not to drag us into a barn at the crack of dawn!"

Aunt Juicy loved making examples out of the stray cousin who chose to try her. Poor Terry, Tania thought.

Tania took her focus off of the early morning and transferred her attention back to her aunt, who had returned to the platform across from the bleachers.

"I've never heard such whiners in my life. You expect people to instantly fix anything that is mildly uncomfortable or inconvenient to you."

She went on about the kids' bedroom routine. You who don't want to share the castile soap with others will be making soap today. That way you can have a bar of your own. You'll also go to market days with me on Saturday and sell the soap at my booth. Those of you who can't do without your phones in your face every moment will not get yours back today. In the morning, when you report to write letters to your parents and friends; and I mean letters not video chats, I will give you your phones back. Then those of you that can't get along with certain other cousins, I have an assignment for you too. But since you happen to be the most impatient of the group, you will have to wait until tomorrow morning to find out your assignment."

The cousins believed her. She had already assigned some of the boy cousins who couldn't get along, Leonardo and Elvin, to sleep together in a full-sized bed with a twin-sized sheet to share all night. She got the idea when she saw a video of a father who made his sons share a single "get along" shirt when they had trouble keeping harmony. Normally overly competitive, brothers Leonardo and Elvin were starting to tone down their one-upmanship behavior.

She had already disabled the internet in her house for an entire day, separating them from the outside world for 24 miserable hours. Tania recalled how they had picked up their phones numerous times to try to Snapchat, or something. When they started walking past her in the den, making great ceremony of trying to make calls that seemed critically important to them, she had promised to double the time to 48 hours if they didn't stop.

She had already come into the kitchen after two of them had started washing the dinner dishes. She had dunked her hand in the water and declared that it was too cold. "Put those dishes that you already washed back into the sink because they are not clean," she had ordered after the girls drained out some cold water and turned on the hot water faucet. To her credit, Aunt Juicy gave them her permission to proceed when the water was still reasonably but not insufferably hot.

Aunt Juicy had given the cousins many things to complain about. However, she kept them so busy, that they hardly ever had time to complain to each other. On this early morning, she stood across from the bleachers, eyeing the nieces and nephews with a hard-to-read poker face. They couldn't tell what she was thinking. They didn't have to wonder for long.

"Well, obviously we need to start turning in earlier at night. Seeing as how no one wants to get up in the morning when I ask you to." Aunt Juicy, who never asked anybody to do anything, used a loud set of cymbals to awake the cousins every morning at 7:00 am. If someone pretended to be sick in order to sleep in, she didn't buy it. She had techniques to make you get up, and to get you to stop pretending to be sick when you weren't. Aunt Juicy had her ways.

One morning, Tania told her aunt that her stomach was bubbly and that she had diarrhea. Aunt Juicy gave her something to drink. It tasted so nasty, that Tania only drank a little and then asked to lie down for just 10 minutes. Surprisingly, Aunt Juicy gave her permission. While her aunt was in the other bedrooms, making sure nobody was lingering too long in bed, at the sink or in the shower; Tania got up from bed with renewed strength. She was downstairs, "miraculously" healed and ready for breakfast in short order.

"Let's make sure to take our time with those eggs," Aunt Juicy told Tania when she was enjoying the scrambled eggs with gusto. "That tonic was a good remedy for a tummy ache, but don't be fooled by the way you feel. Give your tummy time to heal before you stuff yourself." Tania wished she hadn't said anything about a tummy ache. It wasn't worth it! Aunt Juicy's elephant memory was at work, holding onto the image of that fake sickly face she'd given her when she lifted her head from the pillow to fool her aunt into giving her more time to sleep.

As Tania confessed her ruse and how it backfired on her, she resolved to just cooperate with her "you can't pull the wool over my eyes-you've got to get up early in the morning to trick me" aunt. "Aunt Juicy is too crafty and discerning," she later told Terry. Terry laughed and agreed before he went outside to jog. Terry was a runner and had loved the joy of the sprint. His coach had not taken his running dedication seriously because he didn't like the long-distance running or long walking that the coach required in order to condition his team.

The day after this breakfast encounter, Tania asked Terry if she could join him in his post-breakfast run. "You can come as long as you don't slow me down," Terry said. Part of her goal was to find out if he was telling the truth about getting a different letter. However, she was also wanting to tone up her super skinny body and gain some weight.

After that day, Tania always dressed in a jogging shorts and a t-shirt, along with her jogging shoes. Her mother had insisted that she take them, citing Aunt Juicy's gardening obsession as the reason why her daughter might need them.

Tania's interest was transferred back to her aunt, who was still up front with the bullhorn. She announced that they would be gardening every other day, and that, in the final week, they would travel to Virginia to visit The Underground Railroad passages that were used by slaves to escape to Canada. Everyone groaned. Aunt Juicy's reply was, "I can always add more hard work, and give you earlier bedtimes and earlier wake-up times."

"No. We'll act right."

"Sorry."

"Please, Aunt Juicy."

The chorus of pleading voices rang out in the high-ceilinged room. They were all begging for another chance to cooperate and get on their aunt's good side. If she even had one.

"You guys are behaving in ways that make you seem impolite and lazy. You would rather reach over someone's food to get rolls, rather than get up to get them or ask someone to pass them to you. That's gonna stop."

"You mumble under your breath. You're used to talking back to adults. You question adults like they're your equals. You even lie for each other, defend or cover up each others' wrongs and seem to hate to say please or thank you."

Before continuing to tell them about their transgressions, and tell them how she knew the right remedy, cure, strategy for each; she put her hands on her hips and asked her signature question. "What's wrong with ya'll?"

Aunt Juicy stopped talking and zeroed in on something or someone on top of the bleachers. Soon she spoke through the loudspeaker. "Benitta, since you want to repeat everything I say to your little posse up there, I'm gonna need you to come down and echo everything I say to some of these cousins of yours who aren't listening and feel like others in the room will update them on what they missed."

Benitta, who hailed from Richmond, Virginia and had taken a bus and Amtrak to Atlanta, Georgia and then met with her auntie and three cousins from three different set of parents, and all named Jazmine, for a crowded SUV trip the rest of the way, hung her head. She wondered how her Aunt Juicy could have seen her from so far away. While she was wondering, she slid her thin hour glass frame out of her bleacher seat and headed down to the floor. Even with a hung down head, she looked regal in a long flaring skirt in gold and burgundy with a matching sleeveless top with beaded lacy looped soutache trim. The trim, which is fabric cord, was probably an easy sewing feat for her, because she was a master braider who was used to making designs and shapes with twists of hair. The beads, in a similar way, matched her skill at masterfully adding beads to braided hairstyles. Although her trip was a walk of shame, all eyes were on her queenly presence.

Tania admired Benitta's high shine outfit so much, that she could only imagine the details that went into making it. This cousin had brought a sewing machine with her, which explained why she had so many swatches of fabric in her suitcase and very few clothes. This regal cousin received part of her wardrobe inspiration from the 1960's group Diana Ross and the Supremes. These singing sensations wore many gowns that became hot-ticket items and sought-after styles by the women who listened to their stylized music. Benitta boasted of having visited the Grammy museum in Mississippi where some of the wardrobe treasures worn by this dynamic group were on display. She was also inspired by her African roots, as one of her parents was Ghanaian.

The three Jazmines laughed their heads off as they watched Benitta approach the formidable Aunt Juicy. They stuck to each other like glue, and Benitta wondered if they had synchronized their laughs while growing up together.

"Lift your chin, girl," Aunt Juicy told her. She could not tolerate a hang-dog expression or a hung down head.

For the next 40 minutes, Benitta had to repeat her aunt's phrases, one sentence at a time.

"No ma'am. You were gesturing when I gestured, pacing when I paced. I want you to mimic me the way you were doing up there with your Hotlanta cousins. Come on," Aunt Juicy chided her early in the echo session. Aunt Juicy gave her "that" look and then continued talking.

Bennita obeyed. At first, she was soldier stiff and her voice was squeaky. Before long, she was using more fluid moves and had picked up her aunt's voice inflections. Still, she held back a little bit because she didn't want to appear to be having too much fun with it. And she was having fun.

Aunt Juicy was starting to wrap things up. "You try to stay up half the night texting, talking and using social media and video chatting; yet you complain about having an early wake-up call for breakfast. I was hoping you'd figure out that you needed to get to sleep soon after nighttime prayers; but you won't do it. So, here's the deal. I'm disabling the internet and cell tower connection a half hour after I send you to bed."

Groans didn't sway her one bit. After a few more fussy moments, she finished and dismissed the cousins from the bleachers one row at a time like students at an assembly.

She returned cell phones to all but a few. Those few owners stood around wondering why. Soon, one of her servants showed up with sanitizing wipes for electronics and took the cousins with grossed out phones through a hand cleaning and cellphone cleaning ritual. The embarrassed cousins joined the rest of the family outside after that.

They were allowed to run and play outside for hours, after reapplying sunscreen. "When you hear the dinner bell, cease your play and come inside to wash up for lunch," bellowed Aunt Juicy.

Tania spent time with as many cousins as she could. She talked to Benitta first, being careful to avoid any mention of the echo embarrassment she'd gone through.

She ended playtime with her Atlanta cousins – the Jazmines, before they heard the call of the dinner bell.

Everyone headed inside promptly except one cousin. Everyone, including Benitta, was sure he'd be made an example of when he wandered inside on his own precious schedule.

Tania was the only one who warned him. "Boy you're tripping. You better come on here," she told him.

He gave her a look of defiance and lingered by the swings while the wizened, more compliant Tania beat a hasty retreat into the house and did what she was told. She wasn't going to have any part in RayJay's moments of rebellion. Association with disobedience would probably come with consequences that they didn't want.

Gardening Blues

One morning when they woke up, they were not given breakfast after prayer time. Instead, they were told to gather their gardening gloves, and other such items. They were paraded to the back yard to this huge patch of dirt inside a fenced-in area. The bigger boys, like Terry and RayJay, were assigned to bring up the rear. They were carrying these tin tubs with handles on each end. Aunt Juicy modeled how to pick each type of vegetable. Before long she had all the children picking different vegetables from the garden. Tania admitted to not knowing what some of them were.

They picked from about 8:00am-10:00am. Then she corralled them, the fresh vegetables and a few fruit and led them into the mudroom. They removed all their gardening garb and left it there. The mudroom led directly into the kitchen. However, she did not have them go into the kitchen. She assigned them to walk back out of the house and then enter a side door.

Tania didn't smell any breakfast cooking. Like the rest of the cousins, she was ravenous. She went and gathered her things for a shower, and then waited for her turn to get to the bathroom. She had her caddy of toiletries with her, as she didn't want to miss any steps.

They were practically starving by this time, and yet, Aunt Juicy had plans. She took them to the den and her office. When everyone had arrived, she had bundled up their stationery and taken it to her office.

You Get What You Get, and Don't Throw a Fit

When she started handing out pens and telling them that they were going to write their parents, they started whining over being assigned the wrong pens. "I brought a Monte Blanc pen," Terry announced. Others tried to trade or grab for the pens that they had brought with them.

"You get what you get, and don't throw a fit," the frustrated aunt told them.

When they tried the same tactic with the stationery, she continued her message. She was not about to let them rule her in her house. Some of them eyed other cousins using their neon, blinged or special designed stationery paper.

"Stop acting like spoiled brats. You can't always have your way. You get what you get, so don't throw a fit. You are not at Burger King. You can't have it your way." Then she dropped a bomb. "You have 15 minutes to write a letter to your parents and then get down for breakfast. Use the format of the example that I put on the board." At that moment she pushed a button and this screen began to roll down along one wall. Tania noticed that everything for a traditional letter was there; including a greeting, heading, and body.

"If you want to enjoy this breakfast, you will be either early or on time. A late arrival will get you orange juice and toast." A flurry of writing began, with unfamiliar pens flying across paper that belonged to someone else. Everyone had a table space, and they put pen to paper and went at it with gusto. Even RayJay gave it his all.

The older children helped the younger ones, and most of those who had not started school ended up being told to draw hearts and flowers. Tania, Benitta and the three Atlanta girl cousins wrote the "Dear Mommy and Daddy," and the "With Hugs and Kisses" for every little person. Tania noticed that all three Jazmines printed their letters the same.

She intended to ask them if they had attended the same schools. Instead she queried, "How close are your houses?"

"Walking distance," they all chimed. Tania raised an eyebrow and responded with an, "OK, then."

RayJay missed breakfast by a minute, although it was not his intent. He was like everyone else. He eyed the bright pulpy orange juice with suspicion. It freaked him out and made him stutter.

"Why is it this color?" he was bold enough to ask. Everyone else had wondered the same thing, and no one took a single sip out of their glass. They had drank water though, as Aunt Juicy provided it at every meal. It was faucet water, which they also needed to get used to. "What? You think I'm going to buy bottled water?," she had asked each time one of them showed shock or dismay at being asked to get water from the faucet.

"Because it's freshly squeezed, boy," Aunt Juicy said with annoyance in her voice. After this revelation, they started to drink the beverage.

Tania loved the beverage! She had never ever drank fresh squeezed orange juice. When she saw orange peels in the trash while washing dishes, she thanked her lucky stars.

One day their aunt sent Tania and Terry to the garden to get bell peppers. They circled around and looked at the rows of different veggies. "It has to be shaped like a bell," Tania said.

"Well, we know that," Terry responded. They finally found them. They picked six, making sure to get green, yellow, and red ones, then got out of the garden as quickly as possible.

But the next day, when some cousins were sent out to get zucchini, they sneaked and looked up images of them on the internet before going out to the garden.

The zucchini soup and homemade cornbread that they ate that night was so enjoyable. Tania had seconds of both. The iced tea with orange zest and slices atop was delicious and filling. The older girls had helped make the cornbread. Working with a sifter had been a challenge all by itself. They had tinges of white in unusual places on their bodies and clothing that required showering and changing clothes after putting the cornbread in the oven.

"I provided aprons! How did your clothes get so messed up?" Aunt Juicy had asked. She didn't wait for an answer but headed for the kitchen. To her surprise, the girls had cleaned up the mess. They also surprised her when they came downstairs and took the cornbread out at its golden brown readiness.

"I had never eaten homemade cornbread or eaten cornbread with real butter," Tania said. She was stuffed when she left the table.

She bowed out of the evening walk with Terry and went to bed early. She read for a while, having brought a few books, per her Aunt's instructions.

When Tania had her first fresh cucumber and tomato salad, her eyes rolled all around with pleasant delight. Before them was some meatloaf, mashed potatoes, green beans and cornbread (again). The cornbread had been made by a different team of girls, with Aunt Juicy providing instructions and a recipe, and then leaving the kitchen. Like everyone else, Tania enjoyed the meal immensely. She was, once again, spoiling for a second helping of the salad. It was something about this fresh picked stuff that made her appetite spike. This was another one of those days when she told Terry that she was bowing out of the evening walk.

Aunt Juicy was happy to be sought out for information. RayJay had come bouncing up to her one rainy day while she was cooking breakfast and putting food in the slow cooker for lunch. "Aunt Juicy, what did you do before you retired?"

She stirred the eggs and turned to her nephew. "I did several things during my enduring career. I enjoyed my work."

"Did you teach?" he asked. "I ask because you are always teaching us something, giving us a lesson in this and that."

Aunt Juicy smiled. "You are a curious somebody, aren't you?" She smiled again. She made him think that maybe she had worked in some secret capacity.

RayJay automatically thought of the FBI or CIA. Maybe she was an operative, he thought to himself. If she had been, he knew that it had been a very nontraditional career for a female when she was younger.

No matter how much he pleaded, she would not give him details about her line of work. Still, he spent many days tallying up her skill set. He figured out that she could do lots of things and do them well.

RayJay recalled how his mother had often taught him, "In the absence of facts, people make up stuff." He kept the conversation with his aunt to himself. He wondered if she would ever disclose the details of her job.

He ate breakfast with his cousins later that morning, and he thought about the conversation he'd had with his auntie.

He finished early but stayed at the table. That's when he saw Terry put something in his mouth like a tablet. He swung towards his aunt to see if she also noticed. She seemed to take in the details but did not register any response. He wondered if it was some kind of illegal drug. He hoped no one brought drugs, or even cigarettes, to his auntie's house.

He intended to visit with his aunt on the following morning to see if she knew anything about Terry's medicine. He hoped she would talk more about her job or career. However, a servant was in the kitchen preparing breakfast. This same servant served everyone their breakfast while they sat at the table.

"Your Aunt Juicy is at an appointment," he told them. His chin was pointed downward, like he was holding up his neck. In addition, he walked so stiffly, that he seemed to have a rod down his spine. He was dressed in livery, the black pants and jacket rather shiny as if worn often.

RayJay and Tania were the only ones who noticed that Terry wasn't at the table.

The two talked after breakfast.

"He said he got a different letter. He was seen by the two of us at different times taking a pill. He acts like a spy or snitch sometimes," Tania summed things up. "Oh, and he is gone this morning."

The two went back inside the house, which was a good thing. Five minutes later, Aunt Juicy entered the house. Surprisingly, Terry wasn't with her. Tania looked outside and noticed that he was outside power walking. His arms weren't swinging like they usually were, and he was not walking with the same pep in his step.

Terry was lethargic at breakfast the next day, and again he seemed to slip something in his mouth before taking a sip of his fresh squeezed orange juice.

As they were finishing up breakfast, and some of the older ones were clearing the table, Baby Sweet ran up and grabbed Terry's glass. It was still 3/4 full of the beverage and had sweat drops of condensation on the glass. Before she could put it to her mouth, Aunt Juicy jumped up, hiked to her side and knocked the drink out of her hands. The juice spilled on the carpet and chair. The child was reprimanded. "You don't drink after people. What's wrong with you?" The child ran to Benitta and put her thumb in her mouth while she watched to see what Aunt Juicy would do.

Tania wondered, was Aunt Juicy making a mountain out of a molehill? Later that evening, Tania knocked on her Aunt Juicy's door. She had walked the hall for about 10 minutes before stopping at the door. When Aunt Juicy invited her in, Tania sat a good distance away, overwhelmed by the pink and gold color scheme and burled walnut furnishings in the room. She cleared her throat and then told her aunt what was on her heart.

"Aunt Juicy, we want to have a good relationship with you. We just don't know how. We feel like you find fault, instead of finding reasons to praise us, and it hurts. Can you try to see things from our side sometimes? None of us are in trouble at home or school. Like me, the worse thing I do is wander off sometimes. I don't mean to worry my parents when I do, but I just feel like something is pulling at me to travel around the city and check things out. Other than that, I never give them a minute's worry. RayJay hangs with street kids, but I found out that they are good street kids – ones who fell on hard times and are homeless. He told me he does it so he can share food with them, give them things like movie tickets and restaurant gift cards that he buys with his allowance.

Aunt Juicy, did you know that none of us do drugs, smoke cigarettes, or anything like that. We're good kids," Tania said with finality.

Aunt Juicy's voice was soft as velvety crème when she said, "I hear you Tania. I will give everything you said my serious consideration. Thanks for coming to me."

Tania got to the door and saw that her aunt was climbing in bed. "Would you like for me to turn out the lights?"

"Yes love," Aunt Juicy whispered.

Hot Chip Madness

On the same day when Aunt Juicy and Terry had been missing at breakfast time, the two sisters from Boston had gotten onto a food delivery app and ordered up a storm of hot chips. It was a huge variety pack.

At first, it went undetected because they had text messaged the delivery person to bring it to the mud room. From there they smuggled it up the stairs and into their room. There they hid it in a trunk in the closet. They ate one bag a day each, in the bathroom. They smuggled the chip bags in their caddies and hid them under their special initialed towels that their mom had sent from Italy.

While in the bathroom, they would put some chips in their mouths and then hold them there until they became soggy. Only after the chips were too soft to make telltale crunching sounds did they chew them.

For the first week, it wasn't a problem. Then they started eating two bags per day each. This led them to drinking a lot more water because their mouths and throats burned. Their aunt thought they had bladder infections because they went to the bathroom so often.

By the third week, they noticed a few ants. They destroyed the ants and then upped the intake to three bags a day and included RayJay, Benitta, Tania and a few others in the hot chip nightly feast. They deliberately excluded Terry, as he'd become the one nobody trusted.

When the Boston Beauties found an ant trail leading to the trunk, they invited everyone except toddlers inside their room one night.

This is what they told them: "Guys, we have some hot treats to share. If you're brave enough to join us, we're trying to eat 32 bags in the next two days. If you're in, sign this pledge promising to drink plenty of water, wash your hands and brush your teeth afterward, and not tell or otherwise reveal to Aunt Juicy that we have these treats in the room."

They stopped talking and then watched cousins line up to sign up. The three Jazmines looked at each other for a while, and then shrugged in unison. Apparently, that meant they were game, because they got in line, three in a straight row like ants on a log. Benitta was the last to get in line, as she had slipped down the hall and made sure Baby Sweet and the other oh-so-very-young ones were sleeping soundly.

In the meantime, Tania had gone through her luggage and found some plastic storage bags in which to store the unclosed bags of chips. She had smuggled them up to the room later while her aunt was teaching the boys how to sew buttons on a shirt or stitch up a small hole on clothing, with a little help from stitch expert, Benitta. Tania had peeped into the den while this was going on. She saw the boys mouthing the song from "Mary Poppins," behind their aunt's back, as well as the classic, "Doe, a deer, a female deer." However, she also saw the boys get busted as Aunt Juicy swiveled around and caught them in the act.

"Oh, I guess I should sign a certain group of young men up for singing lessons," Aunt Juicy chirped. Tania smiled and went upstairs. She thought of her aunt as more of a Nanny McPhee type.

The Boston Beauties, as they were called, had done some internet research and discovered how to use bugs from the garden to take care of the ant problem. Their solution worked temporarily.

The reason the Boston sisters were dubbed Boston Beauties is that they had funds to take an Uber to and from the nearby city to have their hair done. It went this way for 3 weeks, once a week. Then Aunt Juicy suggested that they invite the stylist to her home to do hair tutorials for them. "Save those Uber fees," she told them. They agreed. Beverly, the stylist, loved the idea and was always invited to share dinners with them.

The Bostonians now knew numerous ways to style their own hair. One Saturday evening, while they were enjoying cold slices of watermelon, Tania asked whether Beverly had been tutoring the girls in Math or Reading.

"I'm giving hair tutorials, so the girls can style their own hair," Beverly explained.

Aunt Juicy spoke up, "Would any of you other girls like to join in? Would you like to participate, Tania?" A chorus of high-pitched voices accepted the opportunity. Later, when Aunt Juicy walked Beverly to her car, they discussed and negotiated the rate increase. On the following week, other girls were able to benefit from the instruction, and the Boston Beauties helped them out. All the girls looked "fly" especially on Saturdays when their hair was freshly done, thanks to Beverly. She had even brought her styling tools for males and had shaved a fleur-de-lis on the side of Terry's hair because he was a devotee of the New Orleans Saints, who used the three-petaled lily as their logo.

"Didn't plantation slaves used to get branded with that lily flower?" Benitta asked when she first saw it.

"Don't start," replied Terry. He knew that this was a part of the historical legacy of the flower, but felt that new meanings for it had been adopted.

When cousin after cousin started having spells of coughing, tummy burns, mouth burns, and massive indigestion, Aunt Juicy had to cancel a Saturday visit. When the girls and boys lay around a lot and were seen drinking massive amounts of water, she investigated.

She saw Tania, the Jazmines and the Boston Beauties outside drinking from the water hose, and their city breeding didn't match the image. Added to that was their unkempt hair. They had also called to ask Beverly not to come.

"Girls, come talk to me," she yelled from the porch.

After some stern looks and no-nonsense language, she found out that they had done some serious overeating.

Soon, she loaded everyone except Terry and a couple of others into her SUV and pointed it towards the city hospital.

While waiting for the children to be examined, Aunt Juicy prayed. She didn't want the children to be hurt while on her watch. She was so nervous. She wondered if it was something she had fed them, and hoped that wasn't the case. She sat there, thinking about contacting her siblings about their children, but she decided to wait. It was while sitting there that something dawned on her. She realized that what her siblings had done is chosen to deliberately do some of their parenting very differently from the way their parents had. As a result, many of them vowed to not be so hard on their own children. She knew these nieces and nephews were raised differently than herself and her siblings. There were some learning gaps because of what their parents chose to emphasize and not emphasize in teaching their children. As she was thinking about this, she realized they had been overcorrecting, not wanting to be like their parents.

"I can't assume that they know better," she said to herself. She vowed to be a teacher for them, and not punish or fuss at them so much. "I can't assume they've been taught certain things," she told herself. She awaited the word from the charge nurse or someone. "I can't assume that the way they act and think is all wrong just because it's different from my own," she told herself.

After examining each child, the emergency room crew gave the Bridge cousins a serious talking to, first in their separate exam rooms, and then later when they were all gathered around their relieved aunt.

"This is fixable, but the children have to lay off of hot chips. They crave them and get a little perk from eating them. That's why they tend to continue eating them." He turned to face the children and continued. "We can prescribe Aloe Vera juice, which your aunt can buy at a health food store over the counter, have you take over-the-counter antacids, or have you drink Pedialyte and even make popsicles out of it. But you guys have to lay off hot chips. No more hot chips." The doctor, taller than any adult in the waiting room, gave them a serious look.

Groaning from discomfort and teary-eyed from their suffering, the children all agreed.

"You could get really sick. It could change your life if you continue doing this," he said. Then he asked if there were any questions. After that, he looked at Aunt Juicy. She stood and followed him to the front nurses' desk. They chatted for a while. Then Aunt Juicy rounded up her darlings and took them home.

Aunt Juicy set up a triage at home in her den. Clad in pajamas and spread out on sleeping bags and air mattresses, they lay within reach of their aunt. She sat up for most of the night in a recliner and gave them aloe Vera juice, which eventually made them go to the bathroom. She also let them suck on Pedialyte popsicles, while she told them stories of foreign lands she'd visited. She waited on them hand and foot, happy that the problem wasn't a more serious one. The next night she slept on the couch in the den and watched over them again like a brooding hen. Baby Sweet, who had escaped the situation because no one dared give a baby something so hot to eat, walked around and patted their faces. "There, there. You'll be okay," she would tell them in a Mickey Mouse voice.

Tania and Terry raised up from their spot and pointed to a place on their faces where Baby Sweet could plant a kiss. She gleefully complied. She then went to the three Jazmines, and as if she could read them well, she said, "Forehead kiss," and kissed them all on their foreheads.

The brothers who had struggled so much with getting along, and who had been sharing one twin sheet at night, were sharing a large sleeping bag. During the first night, they jockeyed for space by nudging each other and pulling at the sleeping bag. By the second night, they were sleeping harmoniously.

On Sunday evening, most of the children were feeling better. Aunt Juicy told them about a time when the slaves had recently been freed, were blessed by a Jubilee when they were just about at their lowest point, and unaccustomed to fending for themselves.

Prayerful Jazmine piped in, "It's almost like the time God sent manna from heaven for the Israelites, or the time that Jesus fed the multitudes. A totally God thing."

"I want to share a story with you. It's one that may make you feel inspired, cause you to know your family history better, and that will boost your image of yourself at the same time. Who's interested?" Aunt Juicy asked. Every child raised their hand high. She saw so much eagerness in their eyes, it almost made her heart burst. She couldn't resist a little teasing though. "Oh, that's alright. I don't want to bore you guys," she said and then picked up a magazine and pretended to read it.

"Please, Aunt Juicy, don't leave us hanging here like the droopy branches of a weeping willow tree," pleaded RayJay.

"Yeah, give us the goods," said Tania, with a twinkle in her eye. Aunt Juicy had never teased them before, and it showed a charming and playful side of her.

She put the magazine down with a flourish and the children moved in closer to sit at her feet. Their faces were upturned, as if to catch every word that dropped from her mouth.

She took on a story-telling voice and began. "Well, the Bridge family slaves first landed in New Orleans, where the slave trade was most robust. They were fortunate to be grouped together as what was known as a coffle. When their master first talked to them, the oldest slave, your great, great, great grandfather – noticed that he had this gentle tone, good nature and a biblical name. So, Daniel caught his eye and said, "Sir, you mean like Jedidiah from the Bible?"

"That be true," said Jedidiah, the slim master who was a bit fond of tobacco. He was even fonder of his mother who named him, so the Bridges were awarded favor from the first minute because of Daniel's insightful first impression. They didn't suffer as much hardship and were not mistreated like some slaves were on numerous other plantations.

One of the things he did when the slaves showed themselves to be hard workers in the tobacco and cotton fields on his vast land is to give each family unit a plot of land of their own. Daniel and other men with families grew, harvested, and ate their own vegetables. He noticed that the Bridge family always gave their children Bible names. Mr. Jedidiah would take the heads of these families to market with him, where they sold their surplus, the crop yield that exceeded what they needed. He let them keep their own money and would have them with him as he shopped the general stores. They shopped while he shopped, and he had warned the shop owners to treat them well and accept their commerce. This self-direction and personal contribution to their betterment became a hallmark of the Bridge family. It continues until this day.

Long after slavery was over, the Bridges have sustained themselves through selling the fruits of their labor. While it was no longer crops, they found many things to make and sell. Your great, great grandfather sold the shirts that his wife made, and the pies that his mother and sisters made. Others made things like rugs, quilts, woven baskets and sewn goods for little babies. They pooled their extra money together like his father had taught him. He was the trusted holder of these funds. He eventually saved enough to buy the freedom of all the Bridge's on that New Orleans plantation. Every male for the first two generations after slavery were given quadruple cadence names from the Bible like Jedidiah, Jeremiah, and Hezekiah."

"Does that mean four syllables?" Tania was curious. Aunt Juicy nodded and continued.

"Even as the family began to scatter, especially after the Emancipation Proclamation, there were always those who found something that people needed and sold it to make their own money. Some of them took jobs as porters, domestic workers, and then factory workers. They continued working their side businesses, and that practice continues to this very day."

The children issued expressions of awe, and then discussed ways they could use their skills, talents, and gifts to create personal income in keeping with the newly revealed family tradition.

Benitta stood up and declared, in a thrilling voice that she used when she became excited, "I'm going to make fancy, high-shine dresses and sell them on my own Etsy shop." Others piped in with their ideas.

Aunt Juicy could see signs that the children were getting better. One started smiling more, another didn't toss and turn as much during their sleep, another spent more time saying their prayers before going to sleep, and yet another awoke earlier and said they were hungry. She did what she did every morning; which is sing, "What a Wonderful World," as a wake-up call. This song by New Orleans born Louis Armstrong had just the hook to make them want to get up and face the world described in the lyrics.

By Monday, the children were cured. They were able to tolerate more activity and food and were much wiser. Aunt Juicy had made the guilty ones write their parents and detail their experiences. Several of the parents called her after receiving the letters, so they could hear the gist of the matter directly from her.

"I'm downgrading their phone service bundle, Juicy. After today the girls won't be able to get on any apps except Grammerly, a couple of coding apps, art apps, and one where they can make slide shows," said her wealthy sister, who had returned to Boston from a trip to Italy. She had not been surprised to hear that her girls had used apps to get the chips. They loved coding, searching for cool apps, and had been using Uber and Lyft ride-share apps and food delivery apps for three years.

"It wouldn't hurt if you could be home more," Aunt Juicy told her sister.

"I'm working on it," was the reply. "Thanks for looking after my girls and giving them some useful knowledge and skills," her sister said.

Aunt Juicy was surprised to hear the words "useful skills" in reference to her teachings. She thought the nieces and nephews were giving only unfavorable reports about their time with her.

Conversations with other siblings yielded similar results. She had been the oldest by 8 years and had helped raise all of her baby brothers and sisters. As a result, they listened to her sound and wise counsel. She had some ideas for all of them.

At the end of each call, she promised to start sending her siblings some videos and slide shows. "I have two little nieces who can help with this technical piece," she said. One of them was a Jazmine, aptly nicknamed "Techie."

For days after, Terry would tease the chip partakers by turns, "Would you like some hot chips?" Then he'd throw his head back and laugh. If the Jazmines were around, at least one of them would start chasing him. But, boy could he run! He always left them in the dust.

After a few days of torture from him, the cousins held a conversation about him after breakfast.

"Maybe the difference in the letter he got from Aunt Juicy mentioned more rules and stern warnings. He loves to push people's buttons," said one cousin.

"I think it has to do with some type of ADHD or something. He's hyper. You have to almost run to keep up with him when you guys walk. Right Tania?"

"Yes, and he takes these prescription pills all the time."

"Don't forget that one morning when he and Aunt Juicy were out together during breakfast," reminded the Atlanta cousins – the Jazmines.

The talk continued, until they heard the footfall of their aunt. Then they scattered like grocery shoppers allowed in the store during a pandemic.

One morning Aunt Juicy woke them up with a bell. It was clanging energetically while she yanked at a thick, coarse rope on the side of the house to cause the clapper to keep hitting the inside of the bell. She had already told them that on days when they heard her ringing the bell outside, they were to put on sunscreen after their baths or showers and come outside. Once everyone was outside, she walked around the porch, eyeing everyone and said, "I hear how you guys grumble about having to bathe and shower with bar soap. This morning I am going to teach you how to make bar soap that contains no perfumes, chemicals or dyes. It is healthier for your skin. "

She circled around them like they were prey and she was predator and added, "You know your skin is the largest organ in the body. You have to protect it, as it encloses everything we have that keeps us functioning." The children waited, thinking she would say more. Instead of doing what they expected, which was never the case, she started positioning them around this huge pot, by grabbing them by their shoulders and moving them where she wanted them like they were giant chess pieces.

"I sometimes use my double-boiler or crock pots, but today, I'm showing you an older dated process."

She told them to put on their gardening gloves. "But we're not gardening, right? RayJay asked. He saw his aunt's expression and decided to drop it.

They were each given this huge block of something, and a cheese grater. She showed them how to grate or shave the huge bars into small particles, and then they placed them in the huge pot. They watched the shavings melt away, and then they were given cups of chopped herbs. They dumped these herbs into the pot while Aunt Juicy stirred. They saw the shavings and herbs melt and blend into this swirly thin oil. Aunt Juicy poured some type of liquid in the mixture, and then had them pick up these little bottles of oils. "This is all peppermint or lavender. Enjoy the burst of scent as it fills the air around you."

She began to pour, like a master mixologist. A furrow appeared in her forehead. Soon the aroma of the mixture wafted through the air and they sniffed in tremendous delight. "Yummy, it smells good enough to eat," stated the little cousin who had tried to drink Terry's leftover orange juice.

"But I won't drink it," she added, when she saw Aunt Juicy look at her over her eyeglass frames. The watchful aunt kept stirring, and then turned to ask Tania to go get a pitcher from the kitchen. "It has an orange flower on it and a handle," she told Tania.

Happy to be given something to do, Tania headed inside.

While she was in the huge kitchen, searching for the flowery pitcher, she noticed her cousin Terry had come in behind her. He grabbed these molds, some shaped like seashells, some shaped like flowers, and some shaped like tree leaves. The molds were a bit like ice cube trays. He grabbed the molds and left the kitchen. Tania assumed that Aunt Juicy had sent him inside on that mission. Tania was right behind him, as she spotted the pitcher more easily when the mold trays were out of the way.

It ends up that coconut milk was in the pitcher. Slowly, Tania poured it into the huge pot while Aunt Juicy stirred.

"There," Aunt Juicy said with finality. She then took the spoon out, laid it on parchment paper as if it was precious liquid gold, and then tied an apron around every child over 12. She then gave them lidded cups with small pouring slots. She then directed them to line the mold tray with parchment paper and pour cupfuls of liquid soap into the molds. She showed them how to move the cup along the molds, without getting too much on the divided partitions that broke the molds into equal parts.

"Pour slowly. Careful now. Good job. Nice. Good steady hands," she told them.

When all of the liquid was in the molds and were cool enough, she let those under 12 place rose petals, thin orange slices that she'd saved from fresh squeezed orange juice a few days prior, or aromatic green mints in each mold. She held her hands over theirs to make sure they didn't burn their fingers and guided them like someone might do to help a toddler "write."

"How pretty," the little ones were saying.

"They smell super delicious," said some of the older ones.

Aunt Juicy had the boys take the molds into the house and place them on the formal dining room table, which she'd covered with two sturdy tablecloths.

Private Meals and Secret Reveals

There were 13 cousins in all, 9 girls and 4 boys. After the first month, Aunt Juicy put out a schedule to start having lunch and dinner in the den with one of them. She called it, "Auntie Time." The schedule was posted on the refrigerator in the kitchen. "My main goal is for us to get to truly know each other better," she told them one night at dinner. "The second reason is so that I can teach you something about table etiquette."

The children shifted on their feet, eager to have their turn.

Tania wondered why Terry was the first one on the list. Then she became distracted, because it was Friday game night, and Aunt Juicy actually had some wonderful board games. None of them were digital. She had games like Hi Ho Cherry O, Twister, Memory, Janga, Mancala, Chess, Checkers, Jacks, Pick-up Sticks and more of those old-fashioned games.

Tania lost herself playing until Aunt Juicy had finished a private dinner with Terry. Afterwards she enjoyed her nightly cup of coffee with a special Coffee Mate flavoring. Then she showered and prepared for bed.

As long as the nieces and nephews had completed their workbooks of summer bridge work appropriate for their grade level, and read for 30 minutes, they could participate in game night.

Providing further clarification, Aunt Juicy explained to them that the selected one would bring their dinner food and drink, on a pretty tray, into the den and join Aunt Juicy at the small round table. There was a tablecloth, a table runner, but no centerpiece. Aunt Juicy said she wanted to look her niece or nephew in the eye as they talked. The child always noticed photos on the wall. Eventually they'd ask about those images.

There were pictures of Aunt Juicy as a child. She appeared, as a wide-eyed child, in pictures with her parents and siblings. There were childhood pictures of her at different s tages i n h er c hildhood. There were adult pictures of her with a distinguished-looking man, including a wedding picture. There w ere p ictures, a t v arious s tages, o f h er with this same man in different c ountries. O ne c ould t ell b ecause images like Big Ben, The E iffel To wer, The Lea ning Tow er of Pis a, Niagara Falls, the London Eye Millennial Wheel and more were always in the background.

When it was Tania's turn, she felt like she had stepped into a vast photo album or a time machine. She looked all around the room and asked for permission to turn on the lights. "Our time together should not be discussed with anyone else," Aunt Juicy told her after s he gave Tania permission. "I'm going to open the curtains so we have some direct sunlight," she was told.

"Yes ma'am," Tania said as she sat down across from her aunt. Between sips of tomato basil soup with a salad and bites of Oysters Rockefeller, her aunt taught her how to open and properly eat the bivalved mollusks using the silverware working from the outside in. Tania listened, having placed her cloth napkin in her lap the way her aunt had done.

They also talked about Aunt Juicy's late husband. Tania wondered why her aunt didn't mind talking about her husband's career but kept details of her own so close to the vest. Tania found out that her late uncle had been a Gray Man, a surveillance operative. This meant that he had special skills in remaining undetected while watching or spying on certain individuals for the government.

At one point while listening to her aunt, Tania was leaning so far over toward the middle of the table that her forehead almost touched her aunt's forehead. She was so intrigued as she listened to her aunt talk about the special work of her late Uncle Ben. She asked questions, which her aunt was happy to answer.

Soon, her aunt changed directions and gently instructed her about the importance of having good table manners, as she'd done with each of the children. "Elbows off the table," she said. She also asked her niece to back up a little bit. "I can see your back teeth, for crying out loud," she added with a tender laugh and twinkle in her eye.

It wasn't lost on Aunt Juicy that her niece was a bit hurt at the way she was corrected about her table manners, so she patted her small hand. She continued, hoping to soften the blow. "It's okay to put your wrists on the table edge," her aunt said.

Tania did as she was asked, and then daintily moved back, straightening her back, to continue listening to her aunt detail the special nuances about her husband.

"He was a little bit like the man from Ireland that played an especially skilled father in 'Taken,'" Tania pointed out.

"Yes, Liam Neeson," Aunt Juicy said. She told Tania that her husband had spoken seven languages fluently. As her Uncle Ben had passed away when Tania was three, she had no recollection of him.

"Mums the word," Aunt Juicy reminded her as she cleared the table. She then put her finger to her mouth. Tania nodded and prepared to take her tray back into the kitchen. As she prepared to exit the room, Aunt Juicy told her, "Give auntie or any host some type of compliment on the meal."

"I really enjoyed the conversation," Tania said with a smile.

"Good job! You can compliment things like the table arrangement, the drinks, or the food, too."

She emerged from the gourmet dinner with a new respect and appreciation for her aunt and uncle.

She was not expected to help clean the dishes for that night, as Aunt Juicy knew the others would try to pick her for information if she hung around there.

Tania went into the game room and had time to join a few cousins in a game of Mancala.

All of the sudden, she saw some cousins who had been playing peacefully across the room, take off running toward them. They were yelling at the top of their lungs.

Aunt Juicy chose that moment to enter the room.

"It's a bug. It's a big bug!" some of the cousins were yelling. Aunt Juicy looked where the braver ones were pointing and went into action. "This is just a common nettle bug. They're harmless." Soon, she had the bug scooped up in a paper dustpan and asked one of the boys to open the door to the game room. She set the bug free outside, then turned and addressed the cousins.

"Okay, let's clean up this room. Put everything away right now, whether you've finished your game or not. Let's have some science, I think it will ease your mind."

Everyone obeyed. Soon they were outside. Aunt Juicy walked around her front yard shrubs, pointing out some of the bugs, and telling the children how they served the small ecosystem. "These bugs keep mealybugs and other bad bugs out of the garden and out of the house." She pointed to a bug that kind of looked like a small alligator.

She kept pointing out certain bugs, sometimes pulling plants aside so they could see them better.

After the tour, she took them back into the house, grabbed a tub and asked them to fill it with Mason Jars from the mudroom. "We'll catch lightening bugs," she announced. It sounded exciting. "They fly around during twilight hours, so this is a perfect time to find them." She had to explain what lightening bugs were to some of them. In short order, she had a good number of Mason jar lids with holes poked into them.

The profusion of stars twinkled down at them from the nighttime sky. They were far easier to see in the country, as some of them had heard. Experiencing it firsthand was a delicious delight, true eye candy. Velvet black always looks great as a background for pinpoints of light.

After the children got an eyeful of skylight wonder, Aunt Juicy paired off the cousins, and had Terry work as her partner.

"Let's do this!" She showed them how to spot and catch the bugs. "We call these fireflies," the cousins from Atlanta – the Jazmines said, as they ran around trying to trap some of them in jars and snap the lids on before they flew out.

After they had several jars full of the bioluminescent creatures, she took them out in the back yard to let them go with shouts of "Goodbye," and "Fly away my friend." Soon the promise of slumber and warmth beckoned them inside, as the bay had sent them a few breezes too many.

"That was fun!" The cousins were breathless and excited as they filed into the mudroom. It was there that Aunt Juicy gave them juice-based popsicles to eat. They were in the den, a rare occasion. They huddled together with blissful delight, eating their cold treat.

"You guys will sleep well tonight," Aunt Juicy predicted. Her prediction proved true. After showers and baths, everyone went to sleep almost as soon as their heads hit the pillow. Aunt Juicy made her rounds, as she often did.

"My sleeping angels," she said to herself. She was happy that they were happy. She thought about what it might have been like to have children of her own, and then dismissed the thought. "These ARE my children, at least for now," she said.

***

The next morning, Tania had a hard time rolling out of bed. She did it though, because the alternative is not something she wanted to risk. Everyone washed up, got dressed, brushed their teeth and then filed downstairs. Aunt Juicy announced that she was taking them out for breakfast.

"Yeah," some of them yelled. They had not eaten out since they had arrived at Aunt Juicy's house.

This is so awesome, Tania thought, as she listened to Aunt Juicy give all the ground rules.

The Laziness Cure

When Aunt Juicy noticed how the children went out of their way to avoid too much hard work and effort, she launched The Laziness Cure.

Here's what she noticed:

When she was at the buffet restaurant with the children, she noticed that some of them sat down and told other cousins what to put on their plates while they sat and waited for the food to be placed before them. She would go and whisper into their ears to go get their own plate and fill it with the foods of their own choosing. "Don't be lazy," she would say as she herded them to the buffet line.

Some of them were sitting in their chairs all slouched over, and a few even had their heads down on the table. She marched over to such tables and asked, "Are you sick?" "Does your spine no longer hold you upright?" The children figured out what her sarcastic questions meant, and they straightened up and sat up or raised their heads off the tabletop. "Elbows off the table," she kept telling a few of them.

Eventually, she was able to go get her own food, and sit at the table with RayJay, Tania, and Terry. Soon, they were eating and chatting at the three tables occupied by other members of the Bridge clan. When one of them wanted something else from the buffet table, this proper auntie reminded them to get a fresh plate and to get their own food.

The children eventually had their fill. When it was time to leave, she made them clear their plates and make the table nice and orderly. "They have..." One cousin was about to point out that the restaurant had people who bused the tables. That cousin stopped short when Aunt Juicy gave her the "look."

Tania noticed that her cousin responded to the "look" as though she had been slapped. Aunt Juicy noticed too and walked over to hug the niece. It hurt her to hurt them, it was like a toothache in the pit of her stomach.

"Sorry love," she whispered. Then she said, "My training and career made me a little edgy. I don't mean any harm. I'm going to start working on me, as much as I'm working on you guys."

Here's what she did about it after their morning at the breakfast buffet restaurant. Upon rising, she stood in front of her full-length mirror and said these words to herself, "Juicy, you're going to lighten up. You're going to stop being so narrow-minded. You're going to be merciful. You're going to expect and let children be children. You're going to make sure that the children have good memories to take back home." From that point on, she said those words to herself every day and tried to live by them.

One Saturday when Beverly was unable to drive to Aunt Juicy's house, due to the rain, the children were corralled into the den. The boys were told that they were off the hook for those promised singing lessons, but she told them all to go find their rainy-day wear.

To the girls she added an announcement, "This evening, after we come back inside, I will teach you guys how to bake bread from scratch."

When everyone was ready, Aunt Juicy led them outside like a hen with a brood. The sunbeams kissed their faces. They splashed in puddles and ran and skipped and hopped in the rain on her tree-filled acreage. They walked down the driveway and beyond, and then climbed a high hill and looked down at the meandering shoreline below. They yelled into the atmosphere and listened to their voices echo down the hillside and bayside. The rain stopped, and they were satisfied.

The hill itself was full of mossy trunked weeping willow trees hanging their green fronds toward the ground like the heads of many women's hair. There were twisted myrtles and bursting/blooming creme-colored cayenne jazmines sending sweetness into the air, spotted with abundant narrow-petaled azaleas. They beheld the.circuitous maze of lagoon-like shoreline below. It was just the sight to remind them that they were in a wetland of wonders. Grass, sand, sky and water seemed to blend into an infinite symphony. All kinds of waterways, such as bayous, streams, rivers, lakes and more were in their view. Various shapes of clouds and swatches of thirsty grasses also assaulted their senses. Down below they saw gulls diving along the waters, grabbing fishes in their mouths and soaring to the heights of the color rich sky of gradient shades. Egrets pecked at snails and worms just under the muddy surface. Rust-shaded rigs, boats laden with shrimp, fishes and crawfish; and their salty, weary fishers putted to shore, leaving foamy mouthed waves in their wake. Sandbars like graves rose to different heights like rounded pyramids or columns in a bar graph.

They focused their attention in a different direction and saw different houses on stilts also referred to as pilings. These structures were sitting atop the water. Those houses shared space with Lilly pads, water grasses and a long wooden pier. Some of the homes were narrow - what Aunt Juicy referred to as shotgun houses. "The rooms are few, and they are lined up one behind the other," Aunt Juicy told them, passing on her pair of binoculars to Terry.

Just then, an elderly lady opened her front door to air out her water-washed home. They could see her moving around, dusting, sweeping and then mopping. Sure enough, right behind her was the back door, with a single square window and tiny curtains blowing side-to-side. "Oh, my goodness! Aunt Juicy you could throw a rock through the front door and it would go out the back door," exclaimed RayJay. He had his own pair of binoculars.

"Or fire a bullet and get the same result," added Terry. In New Orleans, he had seen many such houses.

When the woman opened the back door and shoved something invisible out the door, every Bridge family member who saw it lowered their binoculars.

"Interesting," commented Aunt Juicy, instead of uttering her normal, "hrmmph."

Soon, the children took off their shoes, which at first made Aunt Juicy raise her eyebrows and say, "Hrmph." RayJay used his hand to shade his eyes from the bright sun and looked at his aunt and gently said, "Live a little. YOLO – You only live once." The children coaxed her to lighten up with cries of, "Come on, Aunt Juicy."

After a while, Aunt Juicy allowed it. The children laughed when she started wiggling her toes vigorously. Everyone copied her movements and laughed at the relief of having their feet free. In time, they put on their shoes and watched the skies. From their high perch they saw that a few fishermen were bringing their boats back in, as the sky continued to darken over the waters. Soon, the Bridge's turned their faces upward and let new raindrops hit their skin. While looking upward, a new surprise began to form before their eyes. They soon could view a rainbow from the top of the hill. "It's lovely," the younger ones said.

"Did you know we'd get this treat?" Tania asked her aunt.

"I suspected," her aunt replied. Then she said, "If I could, I would give you each 10 hugs and 10 kisses. MUAH."

"It's like a gift," someone whispered, in reference to the many-hued bow arching across the expanse of sky.

"I feel like if I stood on my tiptoes, I could touch it," said others. Then there was a double rainbow, which drew the most glorious, wonderful sounds out of them all.

"A rainbow is a promise," said the ever-prayerful Jazmine. The Jazmine who loved nature so much, said she wished she could put the raindrops into her pocket. The other took out her camera and took a series of pictures before returning it to her pocket.

"I'm going to find the pot of gold at the end of the rainbow," said Terry. He then took off down the hill with his arms out to his side, as though he were flying.

RayJay, not to be outdone, said he was going to look for the leprechaun who hid the pot of gold. He took off running in the opposite direction.

They frolicked and lounged on that hill until the sky showcased a pink, then a deep purple, and then a dark bluish black. As they walked down the hill, they crunched the brittle scattered leaves releasing this "crunch, crunch," sound.

When the children were sufficiently tired and hungry, Aunt Juicy led them down the hill like a procession of soldiers and into the house via the mudroom. There they shed their raingear. Their shoes made crunching noises on the floor as dirt, mud, grass, floral dander and bugs were shed. They all put their raingear in their dedicated space, using the many hooks and baskets set up inside.

"I guess I do seem a bit like Mary Poppins," she said to Tania, who was walking closest to her. Tania noticed the light tone her aunt used. It impressed her, but she didn't say so.

Tania merely smiled. It was another turning point of their summer.

Vacation Trip

Tania and the others were excited to find out that there was a vacation aspect to their trip. There were only 10 days left before their return to home and preparation for another school year.

They paid a last visit to Grey Manor to visit with the elderly clients there. Terry regaled everyone with a trumpet rendition of a jazzy number. "As upbeat as this was, they actually play this at funerals in Nawlins," Terry told them.

While at Ms. Stout's for their last visit and assignment, Terry shared some more information about the city he loved.

"Most of Nawlins is about 18 feet below sea level," he told them. "It's a seaport city, with great food and interesting ways of speaking. Like the way I say "Nawlins," instead of New Orleans. This is a popular pronunciation of this city. It has French, Native American, and Spanish influences. But a lot of people don't know about the black history of 'The Big Easy.'"

Citing another nickname, he continued, 'NOLA' residents are often tight with the others in their communities. He went on to explain that when Africans arrived in this seaport city, they were made slaves and lived under a rule of law titled Code Noir. He said they persisted in combining their background and their new lives in an Afro-Creole lifestyle. "Haitians also came to Nawlins, basically as refugees." He ended by explaining that the city had a huge slave market, but that some of the descendants of slaves became wealthy." When Terry reached into his backpack and pulled out a box with some triangular shaped breakfast beignets with crispy edges and sifted powder on top, the cousins agreed that the food they enjoyed in New Orleans was uniquely delicious.

"My Aunt Juicy and I made these fresh this morning. They have some of the same ingredients as pancakes, but we add yeast and sprinkle powdered sugar on top." He sat down, proud of his choice of props.

Tania hated to follow such a tough act. She had no tasty morsels to give out. She breathed deeply and began with her signature 4-word opening, "Many people don't know, but Durham once had a hub of successful black entrepreneurs in a place not far from where I live, and from the hotel where we all stayed for our last family reunion. It was called Black Wall Street. Booker T. Washington called some of the prosperous blacks who started a black bank and more as, "black captains of industry." There were a number of financially wealthy cotton mill operators, blacksmiths, factory owners, store owners, and wheelwrights.

The cousins were a bit astonished at this news. It brought them a sense of pride. Tania showed them a collage of Black Wall Street images that she'd found on the internet. They were slow at passing it around, because like the beignets, they had to slowly digest the contents of the speech prop. Captains of industry that looked like them.

RayJay was next. He got up and began spitting out a rap sequence detailing the summer with Aunt Juicy before speaking. "A lot of people know that The Notorious B.I.G. was a rapper who grew up in Bed-Stuy. But did you know-" He then listed, from memory, a whole laundry list of rappers that came from his borough.

"What a memory," Aunt Juicy praised him. He went to his seat across from Ms. Stout and sat down with his arms folded. Then, realizing that he'd forgotten something, he jumped back up. He reached in his pocket and pulled out a baseball and passed it around. "It has the signature of Jackie Robinson on it. He was a brother who crossed the race divide by playing integrated baseball as a Brooklyn Dodgers ballplayer."

Before they left, Aunt Juicy joined in and gave a speech titled, "White Gold." The children and the elderly neighbor were captivated to learn this new bounty of information about the history of the cotton industry.

That evening, Aunt Juicy had them stand against a wall while she marked their height on the door jamb. They each put their initials next to their mark.

Aunt Juicy loaded them up in the SUV at about 3:00am in the morning after directing them what items to pack, and what type of clothes to wear.

The sight of her nieces and nephews skipping to the car with delight and anticipation gave her a deep soul satisfaction.

An electric element seemed to hang in the air like a cloud above their heads. "I believe we're in for one more Jubilee," Aunt Juicy announced. "I hope we don't miss it while we're gone."

She sighed and cranked the engine. When she turned on the air conditioning, the children sunk into the sweet comfort of the ride. Road trip games and activities happened between time-stealing naps.

"I spy," announced Terry. Then he looked around to figure out what he would pull out of the scenes and landscape to finish his sentence. He saw fishers taking their skiffs out into the deep, a deer bounding towards the thicket of trees and a tiny waterfall sending a thin trickle of water down to a splash pool that was hidden from his view. When he decided on a cloud that looked like a storied Navy ship, he finished his sentence.

Everyone had been waiting, so when he said, "something nautical," everyone looked towards the waterways. For the first few guesses he said, "Wrong answer." Eventually, knowing the cloud could change shape or float out of view soon, he started giving hints. "Look upwards," he finally said. Everyone cast their eyes skyward. Soon afterwards Brandy spotted the cloud.

"Hey, it does look like a huge Navy ship," Tania agreed. The game continued, and then they switched to games involving license plates of cars on the road with them.

They rumbled along eventually driving onto a bay bridge, and the children sat up to look out the windows. It was a place where nothing was wasted in nature. Things were changed, re-located or born anew. "I spy, something growing where it shouldn't," Tania said.

All eyes except Aunt Juicy's looked around. Where the strong hands of storms had ripped bark from trees, and scattered them about in the open water like a giant pitching Frisbees around, the bark became home to flowers. The image reminded them of floating Lotus flowers or frogs on lilly pads. RayJay called it first. He then resumed their abandoned game of "I Spy," when he called out, "I spy some things in nature that's been amputated."

The recently awakened youngster had noticed some trees that broadcast the history of the area, telling of hurricanes and other weather sculpting and redesigning things as was common in the area. They sat like different sized students in class, only they were in the middle of water instead of inside a building. Each showcased partially exposed tree roots.

Everyone looked for something that had lost limbs or parts. They soon saw the trees, like headless horsemen riding the waters. Terry spoke a few beats before pious Jazmine, "It's the trees with no upper branches and the top of their trunks missing."

The game continued until sleepiness overtook them. They fell victim, as many before them, to the lull of the wheels on the road, the purr of the engine, the fragrance of the salty air, a gentle breeze coming through an open window; along with the cry of gulls and the steady chirp of insects.

With little warning, thunderheads built up in no time, creating thick greyish clouds at the sky's crevices and cracks. A z-shaped streak of lightening zipped through, pushing through the colors and brightening the layers of sky. Aunt Juicy drove carefully until it became hard to see. The windshield wipers did their best to clear the raindrops, but they were coming down sideways, borne on gusts of wind. She pulled over to the shoulder and waited until the wind softened and the rain slowed and then drove onward.

She stopped whenever one of them needed to go to the bathroom or stretch, and she agreed to take them to a pizza buffet. However, she had nothing but bottled water for them to drink, and plenty of carrots, celery stalks, and fruit for them to eat while they traveled. Her igloo container full of these items was wedged in the back of her SUV. "Healthy food is only a stop away," Aunt Juicy announced periodically.

After several hours of driving, they arrived at Frogmore Cotton Plantation, in a small parish in Louisiana. Aunt Juicy had scheduled a field trip for them there. The main component was an experience with actually picking cotton, the white gold Aunt Juicy had mentioned in her speech. After an hour, the nieces and nephews were standing up and grabbing their backs and hips. Some even sat on the ground and groaned. She watched them suck their pricked fingers and swat at different flying insects, and her heart melted. "Let's get back on the road," she told them. While at her SUV, drinking water and eating the fruit and veggies, they got washed up and bandaged.

"Aunt Juicy, that guide was upset that you stopped early. I don't think you will get a refund," RayJay told her. To which she replied, "I know, but I couldn't stand to see you guys suffer any longer. I'm the boss, Applesauce."

They were on the road for several hours, when she pulled up at an Amtrak train station. "I have always loved train travel because from your window you can catch breath-taking scenes and vistas that you don't see from any other form of transport," stated Aunt Juicy. She continued, "We're going to Richmond, Virginia to visit many historical sites like the American Civil War Museum at Historic Tredegar, Eppington Plantation, Castlewood Plantation, and Manchester Slave Trail. "Ya'll acted like ya didn't want to visit the Underground Railroad, so I took that off the schedule. I don't feel like driving for the rest of this vacation trip. Besides, I think you guys will enjoy the trip," Aunt Juicy had announced.

The children had already fixed it in their minds that they would get to visit the network of hiding places used by slaves moving from the north to freedom in some of the Canadian provinces. They felt like Aunt Juicy had failed to listen, really listen. Then they realized that their actions had led her believe that they didn't want to visit the Underground Railroad site.

They filed onto the train in obedience to the conductor announcement, "All aboard." RayJay announced as he stepped into the train, "New York in 'da haus." He didn't look at his aunt, because he figured that she would be mortified. She wasn't. She was getting used to his robust personality. Plus, she had arranged a surprise for him. When she told him about it, she referred to it as, "The gift of a unique experience."

Still, the children loved traveling by passenger train, watching the natural landscape, landmarks, and city-side scenery go by. They loved how trains followed the terrain, with serpentine winds around the trees, flower patches, cityscapes, and other things one didn't see at all, or didn't see as closely when traveling on roadways. Their aunt had booked a sleeper car, which was both more expensive and more spacious. The train even stopped at a few landmarks, as passengers disembarked or got onto the train. The backpack toting teens and tweens reclined their comfortable seats and slept for part of the trip. Then they were allowed to go to the refreshment kiosk and purchase whatever they wanted. Most of them wanted bottled cold coffee; Frapp drinks. Aunt Juicy allowed it. "It's mostly flavored milk anyway," she told them.

RayJay, who Aunt Juicy had arranged to shadow a conductor, only showed up in some service capacity. He was watching and assisting a man named George, who had come from a long line of railway workers. When he first tapped RayJay on his shoulder and announced in pleasant tones that he was the lucky guy who got to have RayJay's company, the youth had taken to him right away. He found out that

George's family had included porters, men who worked on the railroad, and conductors. "I believe my oldest son might be the first train engineer in the family. But you can follow in his footsteps," he told RayJay.

Baby Sweet, whose loving nature was becoming legend, got passed around by the cousins. Benitta kept an eye on her at all times. She was the one who had packed all of the 3-year olds' necessities in her own backpack. She was the one who had stayed up late and braided all of the babies' hair in diverse braid styles with designs that matched fabric patterns like Paisley, gingham and trellis adorned further with pretty beads and bows. She was the one who took Baby Sweet and the other playground set to the bathroom when they needed to go. The Jazmines looked after the other youngsters and had packed their necessities, but they allowed all bathroom runs to be managed by Benitta because she knew how to walk the aisles in the moving train with a tot in tow better than any of them.

At dinnertime, they were served a full-course meal. Waitpersons in uniforms, and RayJay in gloves and an apron, brought their food to them. They were served everything on real dinnerware, accompanied by silverware wrapped in cloth napkins.

Everyone was careful to use their flatware the way Aunt Juicy had taught them during their rotation of one-on-one dinners. Between bites of food, they discussed, and somewhat critiqued the different speeches they'd given at Ms. Stout's during the summer. Tania told them that learning from Terry that Mardi Gras had historical significance blew her away. "Am I the only one?"

Different cousins piped in, with the three Jazmine's looking at each other first and then speaking one at a time.

Nature-loving Jazmine said, "I used to think that Fat Tuesday and Mardi Gras were two different things. Terry taught us that the French term for Fat Tuesday is Mardi Gras. So, now I know better." The Jazmine who was always praying, either with others on an online connection or off to herself in the early morning said, "That this Carnival event begins around the end of the Epiphany Christian feast and ends the day before Ash Wednesday never dawned on me. We were never taught that in school nor was it ever mentioned at church." She fingered the Christian cross hung around her neck by an elaborate loopy chain and stared into space for a moment.

After that, the one who used to use her phone obsessively like it was tethered to her said, "All those costumes, the feathers, the capes, the origin of the name; it sounds like a top shelf celebration of many cultures to me. And of course, there's the beads."

"Yes, the beads, we can't forget those. And we can appreciate Terry for bringing us each a pair as one of his speech props," said Aunt Juicy. Like some of her nieces and nephews, she was proudly wearing a pair of those beads at that moment.

Benitta, who had spoken of the Junkanoo, a similar festival that originated in Ghana, Africa during one of her speeches, announced for about the 10th time that summer, "It's like the Junkanoo, but I don't think it has religious ties. Instead, it focuses on our ability to hold onto our African roots and culture despite the difficulties of slavery, harsh rules for governing themselves, and other oppression over which we of the African Diaspora triumphed." As was always the case, she was wearing a fancy dress. She had told them, "It's a cultural thing," when asked about it at the beginning of summer. She had worn the most elaborate of dresses in African royal colors of blue, maroon and purple, and a nice scarf with flowers in her hair when she spoke of the Junkanoo festival at Ms. Stout's.

Others commented about the two speeches, and then about the experience of giving their assigned speeches each week. Then they started showing signs of being sleepy, with rounds of wide mouthed yawns and stretches. Terry left the cabin for a moment, and RayJay and the kitchen staff came in and removed the dinner dishes. When Terry returned, he stared at the empty space where he'd left his plate.

He blinked as if he couldn't believe his eyes. After he blinked several times, Tania piped in. "I guess you forgot and left your knife and fork with handles at 4:00 o'clock, so they thought you were finished." She was referring to the way to convey to waitpersons whether to clear a plate or not by how you place silverware handles and the sharp ends parallel on the right side of the plate.

"Don't forget the silent service code," everyone chimed in. Terry shrugged and looked sheepishly at Aunt Juicy. She smiled and said nothing. Soon they were all sleeping.

After helping with the dishes, RayJay had eaten with the staff. It wasn't leftovers either, as a separate course of cucumber soup, standing rib roast and new potatoes with rosemary had been prepared for them. The conductor watched as the youth picked up the farthest placed soup spoon on the far right side. He also dipped his cucumber soup from the 12 o'clock position of the bowl and sipped from the side of the spoon. "Well-trained," George thought to himself.

RayJay spoke up during the chatter of hard-working staff people dining in the galley, "I have figured out what industry I want to work in." He beamed at the others around the table, and then went back to his food, having worked up quite an appetite shadowing George.

Tania laid down to sleep while thinking about Terry's presentation. As her eyes fluttered and she fought to delay sleep and dreams, she recalled the way Terry puffed his cheeks as he played a rousing rendition of, "When the Saints Go Marching In," on his trumpet at the end of his presentation. She smiled in remembrance of Ms. Stout and Aunt Juicy standing up with purple, green, and yellow beads around their necks and belting out the jazzy lyrics and clapping their hands on that day in early summer. Before she sat down, the elderly lady told them that the lyrics came from Bible prophecy, the telling of things to come when the end of the world as they knew it occurred. "It's called the Rapture," Aunt Juicy had added.

Tania recalled the image of perfect cultural pride on Benitta's face when she told them that the festival with West African roots takes place annually during what Americans called, "The Holidays," in December and January. With no props other than her attire, Benitta had beamed as she showed them one of the dances of the Junkanoo celebration while an audio file of percussive drums and other instruments played. Before sleep totally overtook her and she finally surrendered, Tania thought to herself, "What a summer!"

For those who awoke hungry during the night like Terry, Aunt Juicy still had a bag of carrots and celery and dishes of ranch dressing for dipping sauces. She had brought them in her faithful red and white cooler. Usually, after snacking, the hungry ones headed back to sleep and to dreamland.

Benitta had fallen asleep with a carrot, dripping with ranch dressing, in her hand. Aunt Juicy took it from her and moved her sleeping form into a more comfortable position. Then she went back to her seat and fell sleep herself.

As they pulled into the rustic station in Richmond, Baby Sweet was awakened by a dapple of warm sunlight on her eyelids. She climbed down with a determined deftness and bounced down the aisle to Aunt Juicy's side. She climbed up onto her sleeping elder relative's lap and began to plant kisses on her face.

Aunt Juicy woke up with a smile and exclaimed in tones of blissful delight. "My, my, my. Your kisses have turned an old lady to mush."

Everyone awoke and looked around to orient themselves. There was stretching and lots of yawning.

Tania eyed her aunt. Her aunt had been tenderized and was making the summer trip seem more like a vacation. But Tania realized that she herself had also changed. She no longer looked anorexic, as she had gained 10 pounds. She had a bit of muscle mass, extra weight, and had gained a rosy glow in her cheeks. She had also gained speaking skills, bread baking mastery, table etiquette skills, gardening skills, and skills at making soap and candles. She could also do her own hair in a few flattering styles.

They got the most enjoyment possible out of each planned stop. Aunt Juicy had booked a limousine driver for the day. He took them to each destination and either waited in the car or joined them.

The Jubilant Jubilee

When they arrived back in Fairhope, Alabama; everyone was dog tired. This went double for Aunt Juicy, who was weary from driving almost 12 hours straight. She pulled into the driveway and awakened the children one at a time. All of the sudden she stopped and grew statue still. "Oh, my." She listened to verify the sound of a ship's bell clanging madly down near the shoreline. It could only mean one thing. She began to vigorously awake the children and tell them that the seafood had arrived at the shoreline. They sensed the urgency, and some even remembered the feast at Ms. Stout's after the early summer Jubilee.

Tania was glad that it came a second time that summer, and that she was going to see it with her own two eyes.

"Follow me," the auntie ordered. Everyone shook themselves awake and went down to the house, where Aunt Juicy started handing out buckets to all the bigger kids, like they were in a fire brigade. She had Terry take ahold of a metal wash bin while she held the other handle in her hand. She pocketed her keys and led the children down to the shoreline. They saw what others were doing and bent down to roll up their pants legs before wading into the water until it was up to their shins or knees.

That same water, which minutes prior had been devoid of fish and had brought disappointment to many career fishermen – was now teeming with fish and other sea life in great abundance and variety.

Baby Sweet patted her hands when she beheld the fishes flitting about at the end of the shoreline. She didn't know all the reasons why this was a good thing, but she knew that it was a very good thing. She reached to catch one fish and put it in Benitta's bucket, since she saw everyone else grabbing fish and putting them into their buckets.

Tania noticed how many non-family members were using baskets to scoop up the fish, or nets to drag them onto dry land. She saw many chasing blue crabs out of the lower position in trees and into their containers. "It's like Freddy Kruger chased them out of their habitat," she whispered to the still summer air.

Tania saw that everyone in the Bridge family, including herself, had mostly fish. Flounder, speckled trout, and catfish were the most common. The size of some of them were the stuff of hyperboles, without too much exaggeration. How could she possibly tell someone back home that the flounders were as big around as a hubcap on a compact car or that they could catch massive amounts of seafood and fish with their bare hands during this time of catch-as-catch-can?

The slosh of the water against Tania's feet mesmerized her, and she experienced a transfer of attention from the present. For a moment, it was as if the rest of the world, the rest of Fairhope, had receded. It seemed like all there was is Bridge family members and their haul of seafood and fish.

She wandered away from the group and started adding other sea life to her bucket. The blue crabs that were further down shore were moving in slow motion, like the Bridge children had been upon first arriving at Aunt Juicy's place. That is, until they found out that it was time for a Jubilee. She found the crabs easy to capture, as were the shrimp and clams. As Aunt Juicy said, it was like the water was pushing them to the top of the water. The fishes seemed to be jumping, their mouths to the sky as if they were happier in the air than in the water. They moved in a frenzy, like springs were in their tails, but not like they were trying to get away from the people. It was so easy to haul them in, as they seemed to be in a state of near stupor. "They don't resist," said Tania, who was used to fish trying to get away to avoid being caught by fishermen, and even trying to unhook themselves from a fishing line.

"They aren't getting enough oxygen right now. That's why they are here. Good we came back into town when we did today," said Aunt Juicy. She and Tania looked around and saw many happy people with washtubs full of shrimp. "That's all some people come for – the shrimp," Aunt Juicy pointed out. "Some people know a number of ways to make it, almost like I know many varied ways to make corn." She bent back over and continued dipping into the water with a basket and putting her haul into her washtub.

Jazmine, the pious one, spoke in a near whisper. "It's like when Peter was fishing and Jesus had him cast his net on the other side and he and the other fishermen caught great hauls of fishes. In both cases, one little thing changed the dynamics and yielded a massive portion."

"This is a fisherman's dream," Tania told Terry as he viewed the fish in great number and the swirling tide. He had joined her, as he knew that variety made seafood feasts more legend. It had been hammered into him while growing up in a city where such feasts came about differently but were enjoyed all the same.

After filling his bucket with jumping, flipping, and twisting sea life, Terry reached into his pocket for his phone. He began videotaping the morning miracle, so he could show folks back in New Orleans how the waters had brought them a bounty. Tania watched him walk along the shore, taping the event, capturing the miracle for posterity.

Fishes and sea life bursting through the surface of the water, schooling together, beelining from the deep into the shallows were so beautiful she couldn't believe it was happening right before her very eyes. The skins and scales of the fishes glistened in the morning sunlight. The tiny waves licked at the fishes, as if to taste their level of saltiness. This made Tania realize that she could back up her story with images, so decided to do the same. She sat her bucket down, and then reached for her phone and accessed the camera. Before she could push the record button, it was over. Just like that. As if on signal, all the animal life from the waters rapidly left the shallow banks and returned to the deep, as if whatever had chased them out of the water was now chasing them away from the shores. She blinked, almost astonished at how rapidly things had changed. It really happened in a flash. In the time it would take to blink twice, those fishes and other sea life answered a call from the deep and marched quickly like obedient soldiers under strict command. They were gone, leaving those who slept late with a belly full of regret that they hadn't arrived sooner or scooped faster.

Bubbles of water with layers of Spanish moss, algae and duckweed replaced the sea life in a matter of minutes; as if to compensate for the absence. But non-desirables can never substitute the desirables - they only bring greater attention to what is lost. Tania shook her head in disbelief, and something akin to torment tugged at her heart.

What provided soothing and soul satisfaction was beholding the eastern sunrise. They all witnessed it in hushed silence as the splendor of the coming day captivated them with its ever-brightening washes of blues, greys, pinks, oranges, and violet in the upper regions of the sky. Teardrops hovered between Tania's long curly eyelashes and her brown eyes.

Birds, who had been hushed a moment before, broke out in song. Calls, chirps, peeps, harsh trills and more filled the air.

Salt and sea waters threw bursts of fragrance their way. Nature's perfume told a sweet story about the morning's events as the waves brought them news from the deep.

Aunt Juicy saw the disappointment and disbelief on Tania's face, and moved near her niece. "Look at our bounty," she said. Tania's warm brown eyes scanned the shores and she saw that the Bridge family had caught more fish and seafood than their hearts could wish. "Terry will send you his video." She called Terry over and told him to share his video with all of them.

Aunt Juicy added, "I'm going to send some of this excess back home with you. I'm letting your parents know to bring ice and storage containers when they come pick you up. At least for those of you whose parents will be picking you up," she amended.

"What a wonderful way to end our time here with you, Aunt Juicy," Tania said as she laid her head on her aunt's shoulder. Aunt Juicy put her arm around Tania's shoulders to draw her closer, and they stood there for a time in that sweet embrace. Then others came with their bucketsful and joined them after laying their containers down in the middle of the circle. They held hands, hugged one anothers' shoulders, or buried their faces in each other's backs or chests. They were a tangle of love, a wonderful group of dynamically blessed kindred people. Aunt Juicy sniffed back tears and said, "I love you so much that I could give you each 10 hugs and 10 kisses."

"I can't let this moment pass without a prayer," Jazmine said. She said a few words, and then whispered amen as the sun broke over the horizon. Everyone followed suit, agreeing to the prayer. It was the start of a joyously jubilant day.

After they had returned to their auntie's home, unpacked and washed; they went to the shores again and enjoyed a seafood boil with their neighbors from many miles around.

Back Home

Like many cousins, Tania took more back home than she arrived with. She had souvenirs; such as a cute coaster set with fact about Virginia, a picture with Richmond icons, and a t-shirt with the same. She added them to her bounty of 'cache' that she'd found when geocaching around town. She also had candles, fruit preserves, handmade soap, and some of the funds she had earned at the bazaar where her aunt took them. Her parents, who had brought a cooler like those Igloos, took home a bunch of flounder and crab legs on ice. They planned to cook a seafood feast to last two days and then freeze the rest.

One of the first things Tania did after resting up was set up an Etsy shop, where she sold handmade soap and candles. Then she explained to the Jazmines, Benitta, and others how to do the same.

With her own income coming in, she started asking her parents to take her to the nearby Farmers Market, where she bought fresh produce every Saturday. Every time she got a chance, she told people about her glorious summer at Aunt Juicy's.

Tania was glad that she'd learned how to enjoy things with a community of cousins and others. All of her wanderlust for this stage of life was satisfied. She was finally Tania Bridge, with no shrinking, no apologies, and no hiding from the world.

When it was time to register for classes, Tania enrolled in a few Honors classes and signed up for the debate team. Her newfound confidence stayed with her. She was going to need that now that she was moving up to middle school.

Others came away with similar results from their trips. They all were unafraid of public speaking, willing to take a few chances, more socially adept, and healthier all the way around. Terry had disclosed to Tania that he had contracted mono before the trip. "Oh, that's why Aunt Juicy didn't want the baby drinking from your glass. That's why you got a different letter," Tania said.

"Exactly," responded Terry. "Hey, Aunt Juicy also helped me to find out that I needed glasses because she noticed that I squinted a lot," he said. Like Tania and the others, he was glad he had spent the summer with Aunt Juicy.

RayJay and Tania talked for the longest. Tania was the first to bring up their delightful surprise as the last of the cousins to leave Aunt Juicy's. After all the goodbyes, Aunt Juicy had carried her luggage, cooler, and purse to the same barn where they had their scathing experience with Aunt Juicy and endured some of her tough criticism. A few minutes after she disappeared into the barn, Aunt Juicy had driven out of the barn in a grey vintage car with gull-wing doors that opened upward. Inside, there was a gray nail head leather interior that was a living dream to behold and sit in. She moved her paisley scarf out of the way and then leaned towards the shiny car. Then she pushed some remote device that she pulled from the seat so she could open the doors for her dog.

Tania and her remaining cousins watched with dropped jaws as the gull-wing doors opened upward like you would see in an eagle about to mount up and take flight.

RayJay took his cap off and blinked rapidly, as if to clear a million granules of fine dust from his green eyes.

Terry, equally fascinated, yelled, "Sweet!"

Tania stood there thinking about all the ways that this auntie, the one that they didn't want to spend the summer with at all, had given them a bounty of blessings and one deliciously delightful surprise after another. She realized that this summer was a key point in their lives.

Aunt Juicy waved, gunned the engine, and drove down the driveway. She swerved and did a wide U-turn so her car was facing her family, her body leaning into the driver side door. Then she gunned the engine, sped up and the car leaped forward while the tires spit pebbles onto the grass. Soon she was gone out of sight. She was going to the train station to see if some of her methods worked with the get-along brothers. They were going home by train.

RayJay continued talking. "I am going to continue to tutor the young homie, and even take him under my wings," he told her. He went to great lengths to express how much he had learned about many of his cousins during their summer at Aunt Juicy's.

"Me too," agreed Tania. She added, "I came to know and appreciate them more than I ever have at family reunions."

In a softer voice RayJay asked, "Do you think your mark on the doorjamb will be very different next summer?" Tania thought about her answer and realized that she was also secretly hoping to get invited back the following summer.

"It would be good to start a tradition," she said.

***

Aunt Juicy pulled up at the station and parked. She walked to the train platform parallel to the side where Leonardo and Elvin were waiting. She watched them each yield to let the other go first, sit first or have the first taste of their large bag of popcorn. She noticed that, when they were about to argue about who would carry the luggage onto the train when it pulled into the station, they accepted the cheerful conductor's offer to lift it up into the train as a compromise. Aunt Juicy lifted her arm and swung it down, saying, "Yes!" as she headed back to her stylish car and a mystery destination.

Tania called each cousin and talked at length. She had a genuine relationship with each of them, and it was a blessing on both sides. All of the Jazmines were doing a sleepover at one of their homes when Tania called. They reported that they were giving classes on speech-giving, and that 10 students had signed up thus far. "We're getting paid, too!" they said in unison. Tania heard cheering from them, and their voices were blended and rhythmic with soprano, alto, and tenor parts; rather than in a unified voice. Then she heard a single voice. It was Jazmine, the little prayer warrior, "Three of our students are older than us. College students."

Aunt Juicy continued calling each niece and nephew and discussed their summer together. At the beginning, she thanked them for gracing her home with their presence. Tania thought she would get a stern lecture on history and a rebuke for flaking out at the cotton plantation. But she didn't get any of that. "You glowed up," Aunt Juicy told her, using one of RayJay's urban terms that meant Tania had made an incredible transformation.

"And it wasn't just a coinkidinky," Tania said, meaning coincidence. At the end of the conversation, Aunt Juicy again thanked her for coming and then asked, "Did you learn anything this summer?" As was the case with the other nieces and nephews, she got all the answers she ever wanted.

Epilogue:
The Fate of the Bridge Family

Years passed, and the nieces and nephews went back to Aunt Juicy's every summer until it was time for each to go off to college. There was always a great send-off for such college-bound cousins. When it was Terry's turn, Aunt Juicy teasingly roasted him. He loved every delicious minute of it. When it was Tania's turn, Aunt Juicy talked about the transformation of Tania during that first summer, and how Tania was key in helping her to lighten up and see her nieces and nephews in a different, more gentle light.

They went up to stay with their aunt for Christmas one year and were delighted to find out that Aunt Juicy truly kept the Christ in Christmas. They listened to Christmas carols, sang many of them around the piano while their aunt or one of them played an instrument, went to church often, served the poor, and read Bible verses about the birth of Christ.

Every year at Christmas, Aunt Juicy bought abundant gift cards and gifts for them from three businesses. She explained that she chose Hobby Lobby due to their pursuit of a Christian culture. She said she'd found out that it was a company that has experienced success by following Biblical precepts.

She also loaded them down with gift cards from Chick-Fil-A, because its corporate culture states that the reason the business exists is, "To glorify God by being a faithful steward of all that is entrusted to us."

They got new wardrobe pieces from Forever 21, who has the verse from John 3:16 on the bottom of their bags. Aunt Juicy had told them that founder, Jo Won Chang, informed CNN in 2012 that he was sharing the message of God's love as demonstrated by allowing His Son, Jesus, to suffer a brutal crucifixion.

87

"I'm very intentional about shopping only from these companies, it's hopefully going to go down as part of my legacy."

They enjoyed the miracle of the seafood Jubilee at least once per summer and drove around the neighborhood giving away freshly caught fish and seafood to others who hadn't made it to the shores in time. As always, they also had a seafood boil or two, and a fish fry where they invited others to come and share.

But, this last visit to Aunt Juicy's was different.

Terry stepped up to the door of Aunt Juicy's house to let the black-clad family inside. She had passed away peacefully in her sleep a week prior, with all siblings, nieces and nephews around her. Baby Sweet, now the age Tania had been during that first summer, was lovingly cradling her in her arms and planting butterfly kisses all over her face as she took her last breath. All three Jazmines were praying out loud, and the rest of the family were singing, "When the Saints Go Marching In." Aunt Juicy had clutched the Mardi Gras beads Terry had given her during the first summer and went to be with the One in whom she had put her faith and trust since age 9.

Once inside the still quiet house, Terry opened the blinds to let the sunshine in, and then had everyone sit at the kitchen table where they had shared many meals. He opened a white baker's box and drew out the huge King Cake inside. He then turned away from them, leaving his cousins to enjoy the New Orleans' delight. Every slice Tania made released the heavy aroma of coffee and cinnamon and revealed fruit and cream cheeses in abundance. RayJay bit into his piece without delay. He soon bit into the signature King Cake baby, a plastic cherub-like baby that signified good fortune and prosperity for the person who had this hidden in their slice.

Terry continued down the dark hallway and into an interior room to retrieve the treasure box that Aunt Juicy had described in her last letter to him. Per her instructions, he didn't open it until he was sitting before everyone. He took a key out of his pocket and inserted it into the treasure box key slot. When he opened the lid, the aroma of roses was released into the air. It had been her signature fragrance, they recalled at once.

Inside there was a pearl encrusted keychain with gold trim. Benitta reached across and took it, clutching it to her chest possessively. Nobody protested this territorial gesture. RayJay laughed and said, "Remember when our text, toggle and tweet reality used to offend or confuse Aunt Juicy? Remember when I told someone on the phone that I would hit them back and she thought we were going to fight?" Everyone laughed solemnly.

Tania thought about the ways she'd bloomed and blossomed while at Aunt Juicy's house. Her auntie had opened up a new horizon of knowledge and experience for them. "She unlocked for us new ways of thinking, seeing, and experiencing the world with our eyes fully opened," she told them.

Terry spoke up, "Yep, she was a plate-spinning coordinator of many things awesome."

Inside the box was a letter for each niece and nephew. There was an additional letter, that Terry began to read out loud, also per Aunt Juicy's instructions.

Dear loved ones,

I'm writing this letter to clear up the mysteries of my life that I chose to not reveal while I was alive. I had my own reasons for doing that. I know you guys wondered where I obtained such a versatility of skills. I was an Operative with the U.S. government for 30 years. I sometimes had to work undercover in "pretend" careers as part of our investigations. This required that I take classes and workshops so that I could convincingly carry out the pretend role. For example, I had to learn how to operate as a seamstress in order to investigate child labor and deplorable work conditions in secret sewing mills. I had to learn higher level math in order to investigate a money laundering scandal. I had to take classes in undersea diving in order to help recover treasures buried at sea during pirate raids that were common in the open seas. I took classes in soap-making in order to work in the remote jungles of one country and had to scale down to a basic, survivor mode existence in order to catch poachers of endangered species. I could go on, but I am sure you get the picture.

You probably also wondered why I was so hard on you, and why I sought to teach you a variety of the skills that I obtained in my secret career. I had four reasons. The first reason is that I wanted to help guide you to the true treasures of life, because you had such a tight grip on things. All of these things you valued will eventually rust, fade away, become obsolete and leave you hanging, disappointed and empty. The best treasure is found in a faith in Jesus Christ, who has prepared a special place for those who love Him. "For where your treasure is, there your heart will also be." Matthew 6:21. That's why I asked all of your parents to get you into good Bible-believing, Jesus-exalting churches once you returned home after that first trip. God doesn't mind you having things, He doesn't want things to have you. He wants to be first in your life.

The second reason is that I grieved to think that you wouldn't have the stamina, resilience, and ability to make it in this global economy and troubled world if you were raised in the dark and coddled by your parents.

The third reason is that I wanted to prepare you to raise strong, righteous children that would be like olive plants around your dinner table. I always had your best interest in mind. I was there at the birth of every single one of you and fell deeply in love with you at first sight. I knew I couldn't have children of my own, so I made a vow to you as you slept in my brother or sisters arms that I would be with you, serve you, teach you, and help prepare you for all that was to come down your timeline. I also claimed you for the kingdom of God and the Son whom He loves.

For my fourth reason, I will share my guiding Scripture. It's found in Titus 2:3-5a where it reads, "Likewise, teach the older women to be reverent in the way they live, not to be slanderers or addicted to much wine, but to teach what is good. Then they can urge the younger women to love their husbands and children, to be self-controlled and pure, to be busy at home, to be kind."

I know I was known mostly as a bossy old lady, but I was also a Christian, doyenne and woman of my word. I hope you believe that I kept my promise to myself and fulfilled the Titus Woman model.

Lovingly,

Aunt Juicy

Terry turned the paper around so that everyone could see the dozens of hugs and kisses she included at the bottom of the letter by way of Xs and Os. He counted them, and there was exactly 10 of each for them all.

BOOK CLUB DISCUSSION QUESTIONS

1. In the chapter titled, "Aunt Juicy's Rant," and, "You Get What and Don't Throw a Fit," Aunt Juicy stressed letter writing in place of the various menu of digital contact systems available to the kids. What advantage was she trying to provide? What are reasons why this was so important to her? How might we/you "sell" the idea to the youth in your orbit or realm of influence?

2. In the chapter titled, "Hot Chip Madness," it states that the children were cured. Besides being medically cured, what else could the term mean?

3. In the chapter titled, "Hot Chip Madness," Aunt Juicy used the nieces and nephews' sickness and downtime to share the family's history. What parallels are there for us in a world/country on downtime due to the coronavirus?

4. What do the children teach Aunt Juicy? Find at least 3 examples that she was on the receiving end of "lessons?"

5. Find 3 instances when Aunt Juicy softened through words/actions or both.

6. Opinion Question: Did Aunt Juicy seem too harsh under the circumstances or make mountains out of molehills?

7. The Jubilee is well-documented in literature, records and videos. Find something to share through research that shows how this event unfolds in the Bay Area of Alabama.

8. What did the family's experience with the Jubilee remind you of related to your own family?

Excerpt

Come Through, Benitta

I grew up with a Christian daddy, Mr. Zechariah Bridge, who often consoled me during sad times by saying, "God places your tears in a bottle, Psalm 56:8. He is aware of every experience you encounter that makes you cry." My mother, a doctorate Ghanaian student who he met at the university, said a similar thing. "Cry if you have to, not a moment late. For if you don't cry enough every year to fill at least one drinking gourd, your sadness and grief will show up in a less healthy way."

I'm Benitta, one of Aunt Juicy's many nieces of pride and joy. My parents had a strong influence o n m e. I w as i mprinted w ith a l ove g ift an d pa ssion fo r se wing fr om my early childhood. I was surrounded by a loving extended family. It was my cousin Tania and Aunt Juicy who put the finishing t ouches o n m y l ife. It s tarted d uring a s ummer w hen I w as 12, when my cousins and I spent a whole summer at Aunt Juicy's country home. I had packed very few clothes, included everything my aunt asked me to bring, and then put many swatches of patterned fabric into my suitcase so I could sew summer wear while I was at my aunt's house. I had verified that she had a sewing machine that I could use.

My cousins and I didn't know we were in for such rich experiences, great influences and soul enlarging encounters when we found out we had to go to Fairhope, Alabama to stay with this aunt. We didn't know what a gift she was to the family until we looked at her with fresh eyes during that first summer.

My hands and days are now full because I'd won a sewing project contest. Being chosen was something that I would have never dreamed possible. I was selected to sew a dress for a special lady who is as widely known as Michelle Obama, as beautiful in body and face as Beyoncé, as well read and successful as Oprah and as regal and classy as the late Lena Horne.

When watching, "The W iz," w ith t he s uper t alented c ast, I l oved h ow t his r aspy voiced legend carried her role. Of course, I was enthralled with Diana Ross and the other iconic actors as well.

I am living in my own loft apartments, being independent and away from my parents' home for the first time. Well, maybe not the first time, as I had spent some summers away from them. I still lived in the same city with them, which they loved. They called before they came over, but they came over often. We'd h ave d ishes p opular i n G hana, s oul f ood, a nd e verything in between.

My summers with Aunt Juicy created in me a desire to design clothes on a higher level than ever before, to do it with a spirit of excellence, and to bring back the Diana Ross and The Supremes' high shine gown look twinned with clothing akin to that which women wear in Ghana. While I was at Aunt Juicy's she noticed and then praised my skills with needles, thread, and hair. She let me sit in and act as a tutor when she taught the boys some sewing secrets and shortcuts.

Because my Ghanaian mom taught me how to add delicious elements like satin florets, beading, detailed mini-stitches and soutache trim to my designs - I felt equal to any contestant in the running for this honor. After a f ew r ounds o f f ulfilling sm all de sign as signments, I was chosen for a celebrity gown design task out of over 1,000 design candidates. Many of the women with whom I competed had attended design schools, institutes, academies and universities to study fashion and design.

I had none of that. I had a passion for design and I had my mom. When I was a wee girl and in elementary school, she sewed all my clothes. I didn't know what it was like to have a store bought dress until I got a job at a dress shop when I was in high school. I used my own money to shop and buy off-the-rack clothes. Even then I had to make alterations. After the newness of shopping like that wore off, I started buying fabric and making my own clothes. They voted me Best Dressed for 3 out of 4 years of my high school days.

When I spoke to the client during the elimination round, I told her about my mother, who often sat me on a stool, and put fabric on my lap and a needle and thread in my hands during my childhood. "She started me on this journey when I was but three years ago," I told her. "*Stitch* and *tuck*," were the first onomatopoeias I learned," I added.

In addition to some of my designs, I showed her pictures of myself and my mother sporting matching dresses that we had made, picture of the gown I designed for my prom, and pictures of clothes I had made for clients when I was in high school and after.

Even my mom had some professional training as a seamstress. She and my aunt in Boston had taken many intense classes on clothing design, sewing with textiles, and more. Plus, my mother had 30 years of experience designing clothes, creating patterns for clothes that she would later make, and fashioning knock-offs of popular styles of clothing under her belt.

I had none of that. But I did have Aunt Juicy. She inspired me to believe for the impossible. Now, here I am living my dream.

~ ~

www.ingramcontent.com/pod-product-compliance
Lightning Source LLC
Chambersburg PA
CBHW070634120726
47909CB00004B/1437